TRANSLUCENCE

BEN DEIGHTON

World Castle Publishing, LLC
Pensacola, Florida
Copyright © Ben Deighton 2017
Paperback ISBN: 9781629898063
eBook ISBN: 9781629898070
First Edition World Castle Publishing, LLC, October 30, 2017
http://www.worldcastlepublishing.com

Licensing Notes

Cover: Karen Fuller
Editor: Maxine Bringenberg

CHAPTER 1

There are some among us whose minds look beyond the electronic filaments that arc across the sky, beyond even the pale light of the stars. Reuben Brunner was one such person, and as he grew to know the world around him, he kept watch over a deep sense of unease. It started out as a melancholy that would catch him in the quiet moments as he lay on the edge of sleep or wandered alone in the adolescent evenings. But it would soon mature into a feeling of detachment that drove him through college, and with the luck of those who don't seem to care, he found himself in work, in a good job. And then, one wet autumnal afternoon, it crystallized into a compulsion to act that was going to change the world forever.

***

3

He'd called her at work, his voice strained and breathless. Alma didn't know why he wanted to meet so suddenly and, unnerved, she'd made her excuses and crossed the city to meet him.

"It's like the two facing mirrors of an elevator, reflecting the image of each other infinitely, a reflection of a reflection of a reflection." The rain against the cafe window cast anxious shadows across his face as he spoke. "The intertwined indices, the ebb and flow of the markets across continents, the automated trades, the second-by-second recalculations and readjustments, the billions of impulses…it's the great delusion of our age."

"Sure man, but so what? I mean, what difference does it make?" Alma had never seen him like this, not during the long nights at college, when they'd all sit until dawn sniffing endless lines of powder and talking passionately about things that none of them could remember for days afterwards. And not when they'd all meet years later to drink pints together after work. Yet somehow she'd always known there was something in him, a darkness that would steal across his face in between conversations.

"It makes all the difference, don't you see?" Reuben raised his voice against the gurgle and hiss of the coffee machine behind them. He seemed different now, unburdened, his eyes shining with an unusual

4

clarity. "Every political decision, every person's life is dictated by the demands of profit, the prices of shares. The market has taken control, and no one has noticed." Then he lowered his head, so close that Alma could smell his fading aftershave and the musk of his damp black hair. "Listen I've…I've got something to tell you." They were nearly alone now, and the waiter had begun to turn off the lights and stack the empty chairs. Reuben reached over to touch her hand.

Night had fallen, and the neon shop signs across the street threw ribbons of bright color against the window like luminescent paint. Outside, the downpour had stopped, and they walked slowly out of the damp warmth of the cafe and into the thick drifts of leaves that had gathered along the edge of the pavement. They ate together at one of the corner restaurants, encircled in a small pool of waning yellow light. As they left Alma bought another bottle of wine and their conversation meandered through the emptying streets until it brought them to the darkness of the riverbank.

"It's like the city's unconsciousness, flowing silently through everything, carrying away the things we want to forget," Reuben said as they stood together against the railings, staring into the black water.

"Like dead bodies?" Alma looked up at him, grinning.

"Why don't you go and check?" He grabbed her suddenly around the waist and pretended to push her in, but their laughter died away quickly, muted by the storm clouds that gathered overhead.

"Reuben, what's happened to you?" Alma said suddenly. A cold wind had picked up across the water, and she gathered her coat around her and turned up the collar underneath her billowing dark hair, her navy blue eyes damp from tiredness and the effect of the wine.

Reuben paused, shivering slightly as if he had momentarily forgotten. "Look, I realized that the system tricks us, lures us into a futile pursuit of wealth we can never get. The lie was screaming at me from every television program, every newspaper, the face of every commuter." He turned sideways against the railing and looked out over the river. "I suddenly realized that this is my moment in time. Just before I left the bank today, I made the biggest bets of my life, and set them up so they'll go wrong. They will have to pay so much to cover them that they'll go bankrupt."

"Shit." Alma gripped the cold metal as the embankment seemed to list underneath her. "Don't you know what they do to people like you?" Reuben put his arm across her narrow shoulders to steady her, and for a while they stood frozen like that, gazing out across the surface of the water. Then a sudden shower of icy rain marked the infinitesimal transition from night to dark grey dawn, and he turned to Alma, his face partially obscured by shadow.

"You must go now, it's almost time."

They embraced under the overlapping street light, sadness flowing between them like the cold black river that wended its way knowingly towards the ocean.

CHAPTER 2

The same cold rain gently pushed Theo forward as he climbed onto the latticed railing that ran along the top of the bridge. The despair that had driven him to this point now blocked out everything except the boiling black water of the river underneath him. Theo had always been an optimist. It was in a moment of optimism that he had met Roxana, striding through the crisp winter morning, and asking her out on the basis of nothing but a shared smile. They quickly became inseparable; she would wait for him after lectures, and they spent their weekends in bed, or wandering love-struck in the park as it cycled through the seasons. In spring he brought her flowers, and that summer, after graduation, they moved in together.

At first they were happy, but Theo's obsession

soon began to cast a shadow over their lives. He would work late into the night, convinced that he was on the brink of something. In the beginning she would be awake when he returned in the early hours, sitting up in bed with the lights turned on. But he barely noticed when she stopped waiting, equations spinning in his head as he climbed into the cold dark sheets. She left him just before Christmas, a telephone call on an icy morning. He could still remember the frozen edge to her voice as he stared out of the window at the faultless sweep of freshly fallen snow on the communal lawn. She had met someone else… it was for the best, she had said.

Then, for the first time in his life, Theo was lonely, and bit by bit it began to tear him apart. At first he tried to reconnect with old friends, but the meetings always finished early, with mumbled excuses and unmeant promises to meet again. Slowly he gave up, and sank into the agony of solitude and the solace of drink. He would drink his way through the evenings, and then sit down to work late into the night, the alcohol fueling his belief that he was close to discovering a key that would open the secret worlds of the Internet behind the firewalls and security systems.

The university had given him six months to get himself together, but when he returned, stumbling

9

into the lecture hall late and drunk, they took him quietly aside and paid him off. Theo had been surprised by their generosity, drinking it slowly, sipping it away in cans of extra-strong beer as he watched daytime TV, or sat on a bench in the park where he and Roxana used to walk. Like a ghost from the future, he would follow the imprint they had left in time. And as he jealously watched the young couple caress each other, the words he wished he had said to her rang in his ears and followed him onto the canal, past the warehouses and old barges, and out into the drunken, lonely evenings. They swirled around his mind as he worked through the night at his computer, drowning out the numbers and mathematical symbols, until one morning, as he sat alone in the grey dawn, he realized finally that they had lost all their meaning. The crystalline moment shattered, his unbound despair imploding around the room. He had picked up the remnants of a bottle of whisky from the kitchen table, and stumbled blindly out into the void.

And then, at the precise instant that he stood on the wrought iron of the bridge staring drunkenly into the churning water, two destinies intersected, like ley lines shimmering through the matrix of time and space. As he craned into the darkness, the latticed froth of the water suddenly shifted in front of him, forming itself into interlocked diamonds around two points of light. Two points that made him realize that he needed two algorithms playing out at the same moment, two points that were two ideas, two heads reflected in the water. He turned suddenly as a hand rested on his shoulder, and looked into two navy blue eyes.

"Hold on." The red lips were exaggerated by the paleness of her skin and the darkness of her hair billowing over the upturned collar of a long black coat. "You don't need to do this."

Theo's hand had already slipped forward over the wet metal and he was falling, the water arching upwards in front of him. Then darkness. He could taste the salty tarmac, and when he opened his eyes she was already gone. He lay there motionless for an elongated instant, gratefully breathing in the metallic smell of the rain. He returned home and savored the brittle scent of coffee on that morning, setting to work immediately. The momentary glimpse was enough. The chink of light he had seen through the swirling back water had ignited his mind, and in the blaze he forged a key; a burnished elegance of interlocking formulas that would dissolve the oblique walls of data that bounded the digital world.

It was almost dark outside when he had finished, and his mind was warped with hunger and exhaustion, but he could not contain himself. He prepared the software that would carry the code out across the network, and then set it to work immediately, pointing it to Roxana's email account. The room began to fill with warm orange light from the streetlamps outside as it cut away the layers of encryption. Through his exhaustion, Theo finally peered at the words she had written about him, and learned that she had lied, that she hadn't met anyone else. The nauseating mix of elation and sadness drove him from the pool of light by the computer screen across to the sofa. He pulled his coat over his body, rolled a cushion under his head, and sank gratefully into sleep.

He dreamed that he had just missed her, her coat tails disappearing around the corners of endless alleyways, a blurry face in the window of a departing train. When he awoke it was still dark, and he stood shakily, stiff from the unforgiving contours of the sofa. He showered absent-mindedly, his thoughts still swirling across the digital landscape he had unlocked. When he had dressed again, Theo stepped out onto the sodium-yellow street in search of food. It was late, and he headed for the all-night takeaway.

As he stood and ate among the taxi drivers and clubbers, a sense of unreality began to coalesce in his mind; he could not tell if he had slept for a few hours or for a whole day. After he had finished eating, Theo wiped the sweet sauce from his week-long beard and stepped uncertainly from the neon light. A cold wind had started to blow along the street, sending discarded pieces of plastic and old wrappers skating along the road. He kicked at a crumpled plastic water bottle as it spun past, and pulled the hood of his old army jacket over his head to block out the cold. Then he turned back into the tunnel of darkness that led through the sleeping terraces to his flat.

He knew something was wrong immediately... the slatted light cast a warning pattern of orange and black across the paving stones. Theo paused in the semi-darkness, panicking, as two silhouettes rose and shrank on the surface of the blinds, moving backwards and forwards across his living room. "What the hell?" The words coiled away from him like spirits in the cold air. Then, after pausing for a moment outside his window, he retreated into the electrified night, fear vibrating in his mind like a sound just out of audible pitch. "They must have known, they must have seen it. They, who?"

The dark streets offered neither answers nor reassurance as he spiraled desperately outwards until he saw the warm glow of the underground station. Theo's hands were shaking as he stepped into the envelope of light and fumbled with his overfilled wallet, levering his underground pass free from behind a stack of old train tickets. He steadied himself on the railing while he pressed the card against the reader and watched the unblinking red light, waiting for the machine to signal its acceptance. But his bunched fingers began to grow numb against the cold metal. It was taking too long, something was wrong. The solitary light began to blink rapidly at him as if it was trying to tell him something. Unnerved, he was just about to pull away and flee when the light finally slipped across to green and the plastic barrier swung clear.

The platform was deserted except for the cameras, which watched him push himself up against the rounded tiles. He shivered as he thought back over the night's events. Someone had seen him move across the Internet, peeling back the onion-skin layers of security. They had moved fast…he was away from the flat for less than an hour, unless they had been watching him anyway. But then, how was it that he had managed to get away so easily?

The troubling thought was broken by the sound of footsteps on the tiled floor, and Theo glanced along the platform at the figure who had joined him in the station. A pair of square glasses reflected the yellow lights back at him as the man looked up, his face partially obscured by a hood. Then the air between the two men filled with the scream of an approaching train, and Theo's thoughts dispersed in the warm breeze. He stepped, relieved, into the carriage and sat in the corner, leaning against the soft plastic as the doors closed and the black walls of the tunnel were drawn across the window.

Theo pondered his distorted reflection in the glass opposite as the train thundered into the city. Judging by the way their shadows had moved, the intruders in his flat weren't looking at the computer, he thought. They must have been trying to learn about him, but what for? The early morning stations passed quickly, and the carriage began to fill up with semi-sleeping office workers. Halfway into the city he changed to a faster line, and when he reached the center he changed again to make the last few stops to the railway terminal.

It wasn't until he had taken a position in the center of the carriage that he saw him again. Two glowing square eyes looking up momentarily from under a grey hood before turning quickly away. Theo's heart lurched in time with the rattling train as he stared, panicking, at the side of the man's head. He began to push his way backwards along the carriage. When he reached the small door at the end, he tore it open and stood for a desperate moment in the howling wind of the tunnel. Then he looked back, but the draft of air splayed his hair across his eyes, blinding him. When he pushed it aside he could see the man walking directly towards him. Then the tunnel fell away, and Theo looked up at the blurred colors of the platform, the speed of the train merging the waiting people into one. As the faces began to form out of the colored mass, he jumped.

For an instant, the world became a sphere of abstract shapes as Theo turned in the air. Then the platform materialized in front of him with a lip-splitting crack, the metallic taste of blood seeping into the screaming station around him. He scrambled to his feet and began to run, and as he pushed his way through the crowd and up the stairs, an unexpected sense of peace fell over him. The train doors thudded open behind him as he reached the escalator, the sound driving him up the metal steps three at a time, his eyes fixed on the disc of daylight at the top. He cleared the ticket barrier in one, kicking his foot off from the top of the plastic gate, and felt suddenly joyous as he emerged in the cool morning light.

Theo turned away into the back streets, weaving haphazardly through alleyways and along the loading areas of shops. Finally he paused for breath, hands on his knees beside the peeling black paint of an unmarked door, plumes of condensation billowing into the still, cold air. He listened intently for the sound of running feet, but none came, and after a while he pulled his hood back over his head to obscure his face and stepped out into the thick city-center crowd. He kept his head bowed while he walked, surprised by a sudden sense of freedom, and cast his mind back to what seemed like another person moving terrified through the pre-dawn streets. He followed this other self as he replayed his pathway, away from the late-night snack bar and out into the deserted, suburban darkness. Then he watched himself step into the orange light of the underground station, and peered over his shoulder while he fumbled with his wallet and stood anxiously waiting until the barriers opened in front of him.

Rewind, he thought, replaying again the longer-than-usual delay, the odd flickering light on the display, the cold that had numbed his hands as he waited prone against the gate. He pulled the train card out of his wallet again, letting a couple of the old tickets spiral to the ground behind him, and ran his eye around the edge until he came to some small writing embossed into the bottom corner... Transcom. His eyes passed back and forth over the word. "Transcom." Theo repeated the word to himself under his breath several times while he formed his plan.

On the opposite side of the street a row of up-market boutiques threw rich, gold-colored light out across the pavement. He turned towards them, cutting directly across the bow wave of a slowing bus. He jumped the final yard to the far curb and entered one of the gleaming stores in a single, fluid movement. Theo was a good deal scruffier than the other customers, and the security guard eyed him suspiciously as he pretended to browse the floodlit shelves. But after a few minutes the guard grew bored and turned his attention elsewhere, and Theo set to work, thrusting a power cable deep inside his pocket and positioning himself carefully in front of an illuminated display cabinet where a row of laptops hummed quietly, geometric patterns dancing across their screens. A woman in a grey business suit had joined him in the aisle, and he ran his fingers impatiently along plastic cases as he waited for her to turn away. Then, as soon as she crossed to the next display, Theo gripped one of the machines on both sides, his heart jumping as he rested his finger on the black plastic disc that attached the computer to the security system, and tore it free.

The alarm seemed to fill the shop gradually as he ran, like a slow-motion explosion behind a film character. He pushed the security guard aside with unexpected ease and leapt through the doorway, diving joyously into the crowded street. The guard only made a half-hearted attempt to follow, and Theo soon slowed to a brisk walk, clutching the laptop underarm. He had run blindly, but his unconscious mind seemed to have guided him anyway, and he now found himself under the concrete mezzanine of the railway terminal. He stepped quickly through one of the arches and pulled his hood low over his face. Then he sat with his back against the yellowed wall and logged on to the network.

Transcom...the word now pulsated in his mind like a war drum as he released his software into the electronic mist, the jangling world of the station fading away. The code cut away the layers of security that surrounded the company servers, and the software began to prowl through the network, feeding him data. He pushed his way through the contracts, the accounts, and the meaningless columns of numbers cascading in front of him. The thrill of the counterattack undimmed, he headed upstairs, slipping into the private email account of the company's chief executive. Then he stopped, his breath suspended, as his search suddenly found its mark.

The words hovered in front of him on the screen as the code waited. Theo's eyes stumbled across them in his excitement. Who would pay to access the data from the security cameras and ticket terminals? Who was hunting him? The cash had been collected by an unnamed man and handed over in a parking lot, the document said. Theo forwarded the email to one of the city newspapers, and then released the software again. The message had come from a temporary webmail address, but the code found the scent, and the faraway sounds of the station urged him on as he sat against the cold tiles, hunched over the machine. As the software fanned out across the network, it picked up similar emails to the police, the security services, the government.

Theo breathed hard. Whoever was following him would be able to track his movements right across the city. He looked up at the grey faces that passed unknowingly through the mid-morning bustle, and then his gaze passed behind them, along the tiled walls of the station. Sure enough one...no, two cameras were trained on him now from the concrete rafters. Theo willed the software on while he still had time, but it had reached a blank website, a dead end.

As he stared at the dark screen, he became suddenly aware of the reflection looking in. He gazed into the dark eyes, drawn to this secondary, superimposed reality, and his fingers stiffened as he saw the unfamiliar brow line looking back at him, the mocking tilt of the eyes, the angular silhouette of a face, another face staring out from the reflected shadow. Theo flung the computer across the tiled floor as if it had burnt his fingers, and staggered to his feet.

"I'm fucking losing it," he muttered, lurching drunkenly towards the glass side doors of the station, waiting passengers watching him disinterestedly. But as he reached out to push his way into the street he was suddenly thrown back. The same mocking face stared back at him from each pane of glass. The world began to blur as he turned and saw the mirrored gaze watching him from every reflective surface. The crowd had moved on now, perturbed by his madness, and Theo ran out through the main entrance and blindly into the traffic. He ran, looking only at his own pounding feet as he crossed the gleaming city, his mind screaming with fear, until he found himself in the quiet roads of the warehouse district. As he stood there, his lungs tearing at the cold air, Theo spotted a broken window on the side of one of the derelict buildings. He caught his jacket on the fence as he clambered into the compound, leaving a dark green strip of fabric hanging in the wind, and pushed out the broken glass with his elbow. Then he pulled himself over the sill and collapsed into the thick dust underneath. There he lay, motionless, watching the grey light move across the wall, and waited for night.

Chapter 3

Theo could never have known that his actions would resonate across the digital latticework that had been superimposed on our world, that the vibrations would travel along the invisible columns of electrons that encircle us, that hang from our bodies like the remnants of forgotten dreams. He could never have known that they would seep into a world beyond, where rivers of darkness bubbled and spluttered into the void. He would not have heard their echo in the metallic ping of a lock recoiling in its housing on the other side of the city, in the sharp noise that filled the police cell where Reuben had been half-dreaming as he lay on the wooden bench, in the scraping of a metal door against the concrete floor of a police cell.

***

Roused by the noise, Reuben slid his legs over the edge of the wooden bed to draw himself upright, but the abrupt movement gave him a nauseating reminder of the drink from a few hours earlier. After Alma had left him by the riverbank, he had found a still-open shop and bought another bottle of wine. Then he had turned towards the financial district, muttering to himself as the shimmering glass buildings rose around him. As he paced out the long pause of dawn, he luxuriated in the moment; he alone knew that the system was on the brink…he alone knew what was to come. By the time he reached the central piazza, around which the great buildings gathered, the shadows had started to evaporate in the blue-grey light. He flung the empty bottle into the concrete flank of one of the banks and made his way to the cavernous entrance of the underground station, ready to meet the sleepwalking commuters as they poured into the square. It wasn't long until the first few arrived like black droplets from a cracked dam, and then, as the torrent began, he started to shout.

"Get ready, I have freed you," he cried, arms outstretched. A handful of half-sleeping eyes turned to look at the shouting figure, his stained white office shirt hanging untucked from his trousers, black shoes caked in mud from the riverbank. The city was full of crazies, especially at this time of day, and the commuters looked away, their faces blank with boredom. "I've done it for all of you, don't you see?" Reuben screamed, surprised that no one came to thank him, or at least acknowledge his cries. He climbed onto a concrete bollard and raised his voice over their pounding feet. "Wake up and start living," he screamed, irritated now. "I've pulled it all down." His throat was seared from the effort, and he raised his head to the grey sky and shouted something inaudible. As he did so, he slipped and fell backwards from his podium onto the damp paving stones, furious now as the crowd flowed imperviously around him.

Reuben staggered to his feet and turned towards the bank, determined to be heard. When he arrived at the front entrance he fumbled for a few moments, trying to get his pass out of his wallet before dropping it onto the floor. One of the security guards bent to help him, but then recoiled from the sharp tang of alcohol.

"Are you okay, sir?" the guard said, the soft tone of his voice carrying a warning.

"I'm fucking great. I'm the one who has made it all happen," Reuben slurred as he stuffed the cards into his pocket and swiped the electric reader on the security barriers. The guard's voice disappeared behind him as the lift doors closed and Reuben held his finger angrily against the top button. A dizzying moment later he stepped out onto a soft-lit landing and turned towards the heavy door at the end. A young man who had been sitting at a desk in front of the door replaced the telephone receiver and stood uncertainly, looking directly at Reuben.

"I'm sorry, sir, he's not here," he said as he advanced hesitantly into the hallway, trying to block Reuben's path. But Reuben didn't even look at him as he pushed his way past and into the leather-walled suite. For a moment he paused in the shadows and watched the two men craning over a computer screen at the far end of the office, their faces silhouetted against the city that stretched out triumphantly behind them. The clouds had cleared and the grey fabric sparkled with a million points of light.

Reuben caught his breath at the unexpected beauty, and steadied himself against one of the soft leather chairs as his fury evaporated. One of the men looked up and began to walk towards him, while the other continued to watch the screen, waiting for the financial markets to open.

"The whole thing is just an illusion…I had to do it," Reuben said, his voice soft now, his mind clear. The man faltered, pausing for a second, and then continued more quickly, wrinkles radiating across

25

the tailored front of his suit as he moved.

"Just an illusion." He mimicked Reuben's intonation sarcastically. "You think it is an illusion. Do you know how much this will cost?"

Reuben nodded silently, and a sense of deep peace came over him as the door behind him flew open and two guards made their way towards him. They gripped his arms and, while they pulled him backwards out of the room, Reuben could just make out the flickering numbers from the computer screen reflected against the cityscape as the market began trading.

He had fallen asleep on the way to the police station. They woke him only to ask his name and to empty his pockets, and then he had sunk gratefully into the unexpectedly yielding wood of the cell bench.

Now a young policewoman beckoned to him tenderly and he got to his feet, steadying himself against the painted brickwork as he felt a sudden urge to vomit. He swallowed hard and tried to clear his thoughts. Reuben wanted to make the most of this moment, and he straightened his crumpled shirt as best he could as he followed her along the row of blank metal doors, rehearsing his lines in his head. Then they turned out into the courtyard and Reuben scanned the windows, looking for a huddle of journalists, but the dull grey rooms looked back at him emptily. He followed the policewoman into the main office and stepped up to the front desk, where his things lay scattered across the plastic laminate.

"Sign here." A fat hand pushed the form across the table top.

Reuben looked up, confused. "Sorry, what?"

"You're free to go, sign here." The voice rose a pitch with impatience.

Reuben looked up, but the policeman's blank eyes revealed nothing. Then he turned to the young woman standing next to him and she smiled encouragingly.

"That's all, sir. Just sign the papers and we'll give you your things back," she said, her blonde curls bobbing against her collar as she spoke.

Reuben scribbled at the bottom of the sheet of paper and stuffed his belongings back into his pockets, numb with confusion. He was still half-expecting a mob of journalists as he stepped out into the cold afternoon, but none came. As he walked away, Reuben caught his disheveled reflection in the glass front of a newspaper shop, and he stopped to tuck his shirt into his trousers again. Then his attention shifted to a television behind the counter. He watched the newsreader as she talked. He couldn't hear the words, but his eye traced the red line of the stock market as it turned sharply downwards.

The stock market had risen almost every day for the last five years, and he had lied so that he could gamble billions that every major stock would fall today, certain that he would lose. It was the biggest bet of his life, and it was supposed to cost the bank so much money that it would become insolvent. But instead he had won, multiplying the billions and giving more power to the system he wanted to destroy. Reuben kicked the glass with fury, his foot bouncing backwards with an agonizing shudder. Through the pain, he could see the woman's mouth moving as she formed the words which were now displayed behind her, the reason for the unexpected fall that had cost Reuben so much: Transcom.

CHAPTER 4

Reuben was caught off guard as the loneliness of a disembodied voice washed over him like a warm gust of air. He moved gingerly forward through the darkness, and paused again as another, sadder voice overlaid the first. He could just about see Alma's face as she walked beside him across the circle of loudspeakers that were evenly spaced around the room like tombstones. Where at first it had seemed that the voices were trying to sing themselves into existence, as the music rose to a harmonized crescendo, it suddenly felt to Reuben as if the force was reversed, as if the room itself was fading into the void. He looked down at Alma, and in her smile he could see that she was also pulling against the music as it weaved the darkness around them. He put his arm across her shoulders and let her thick hair fall over his elbow as they walked wordlessly up to the auburn lights that seeped across the main room of the gallery. Before they stepped out of the darkness, Reuben paused and looked down at the intermeshed wooden boards while he let the sadness of the exhibit fall to the floor like black ribbons in the still air. Then Alma spoke, her voice breaking the spell that held them on the edge of the light.

"If you think about it, if we are the universe observing itself," she leaned against him gently, "then surely art is the most important thing we can do." Reuben knew that her confidence in the world was fragile, its glue-lines still visible from the crashes of a troubled adolescence, but as they stepped away from the exhibit, he realized then that it bound them together, that it was the reason they had stayed close while their group of friends had gradually fallen away.

The second half of the room was raised a foot higher, and they both took the step at the same time. On the upper level, the light split into fragments as it passed through the crisscrossed pattern of a wrought iron structure standing in the center of the room, the metal dusted in oxidative green.

"Yeah, I suppose you're right," Reuben said finally. "But then it's even sadder that we'll never be able to truly express ourselves until we break free from the prison of numbers that we have built around ourselves." The broken light inside the structure's folded iron walls cast uneven shadows across his face, and through the mottled light Alma could see him slipping back into sadness. It had been a week since they released him from the cell, and he had spent most of his days at home, sitting absent-mindedly in the yard, or watching TV. Alma had visited that previous evening and found him still sleeping, half-eaten pizzas and crumpled beer cans stuffed with cigarette butts strewn around the floor. She had invited him to the gallery to try to shake him out of it, and as they stood there in silence, their thoughts intertwining through the latticework, she suddenly reached out for his hand and pulled him close, until she thought she could feel his sadness swirling in the broken light.

"Come on, man, life's like a crystal," Alma said as they stepped into the final chamber and then out into the bustle of people at the end of the room. "All the perspectives intersect. You've just gotta look at it in a different way."

A painted woman seemed to avert her gaze as the two dark-clothed figures passed through the spotlights. Suddenly Reuben stopped and turned to Alma, his face flushed under the black hair that fell over the collar of his greatcoat.

"No, you're not right," he said quickly. "Our lives pass us by while we are blinded by the delusion the system has forced on us." He held her small pale hand in the darkness as they turned towards the next painting, where a half-naked woman sat on the floor with a noose around her neck. They stood there in silence for a moment as the image dissolved into their minds. Then Alma pulled gently at the rough fabric of Reuben's coat sleeve and they stepped out of the exhibition room and into a column of sunlight, which fell through the high window behind the stairwell. Reuben put his hand on Alma's shoulder to restrain her inside the white shroud of light, his voice softer now. "It's just, I can't get rid of this feeling that even though we are together, we never really see each other." He looked down at her, and for an instant it seemed as if they were completely alone, swathed in light. Suddenly he saw that she was crying, tears sparkling like crystals on the edge of her eyes, and he held her as the sadness passed between them like love.

It was a couple of days before Alma called him again, her voice muffled and urgent. Reuben had been trying to sleep away the incessant metronome of time, but had woken up an instant before the telephone rang, as if her thoughts had somehow reached him through the void. "Can we meet?" she had said quickly. "I've got something to show you." Reuben clambered sleepily through a lukewarm shower and out into the cold evening. He had agreed to meet her where the broken mesh of the old city crashed into the sheer glass walls of the financial district, the blackened railway bridges and red-brick workhouses of a distant era now cast in the reflected light of the skyscrapers and decorated with graffiti art. He didn't see her at first when he stepped off the bus and stood for a moment in the shadowed street, pulling his greatcoat around him against the wind. Then the dark patch underneath the railway bridge bulged and deformed as Alma emerged into the blue-orange glow where the streetlights mixed with the falling dusk.

"Hi." She touched his elbow gently. "I've been thinking about what you said in the gallery." She paused, looking up at the shadows that cut across Reuben's face. "And I think I've got a plan." She turned back to the darkness where she had been standing and waved her arm as another figure peeled away and stepped towards them. "This is Zed." A smile appeared, followed by an unshaven face framed in a mess of blond dreadlocks. Zed stretched out a hand. Reuben paused for a moment, and then reached back, smiling too.

"Pleased to meet you," Reuben said, and then turned to Alma. "Okay." he placed his hand on her shoulder. "So what is it?" Alma turned into the shadowed street, the darkness enveloping her almost immediately. Zed and Reuben followed quickly, and when their eyes adjusted they saw her standing against a wire fence looking out at a windowless building.

"What's this?" Reuben asked as he peered through the mesh at the featureless block.

"This, my friend, is the electricity substation that feeds the banks."

"Listen." Zed spoke so softly that they had to lean in towards him to make out what he said. "First we take their back-up generators offline…that's the easy bit. Then we only have to activate the code in the substation here, and we'll fry everything." Reuben looked up at him in the darkness and smiled. "All we need to do is get into the building, and then fzzz," Zed said, grinning and waving his hand in a circle.

Reuben spent a few minutes scrutinizing the perimeter before he spoke. "Yeah, but how are we going to do that exactly?" he said as his eyes traced the double strand of razor wire that coiled all the way around the top of the fence. The three dark figures stood without speaking for a while, gazing through the wire mesh into the courtyard. Then Alma broke the silence.

"I think I know a way, just give me some time," she said as they turned back towards the tunnel of yellow light.

Chapter 5

The hiss and schlup of the water pipe broke his train of thought as he sat looking at the naked woman engraved into the wall. Reuben pushed himself back against the concrete and glanced up at the smiling face of a young man who had leaned across to pass him the glass device.

"No thanks," Reuben said quickly. It had been almost five years since he'd last smoked marijuana. He couldn't take the paranoia anymore. He remembered his last time clearly, standing white-faced in the street listening to the terrifying drumroll of his heart, cold ball bearings of sweat rolling down his forehead as he stared into the dizzying blackness.

Sober, then. Reuben looked from one face to another. The dreadlocked Indian staring at the floor through steamed round glasses, the mohawked punk frantically twisting the knob of the old stereo, the scarlet-haired Japanese girl as she lit the flared end of a joint, and Alma, whose deep blue eyes seemed slightly glazed through the white coils of smoke. Reuben turned back to the tunnel of his thoughts and let his mind fall back through the past weeks. It seemed like too much of a coincidence that the first day that the stock market had fallen significantly in years was the exact same day he had made his bet, and he couldn't shake the feeling that the system he hated had somehow found a way to defend itself.

It was the same train of thought that Alma had broken earlier that evening when she had stood in the hallway of his flat shouting his name, her small clenched fist banging on the door, shaking him to his feet, dry-mouthed and hot, thick corduroy lines of the sofa still visible along the side of his face. She'd spoken fast, her words stumbling into each other. "Come on, they're going to do it," she had said as she dragged him, protesting, out into the hallway and down the stairs. Outside, Zed raised a hand at him from behind the wheel of a rusted Transit van, his dreadlocks bobbing as he nodded wordlessly. "We won't have long," Alma was saying as Zed rammed the van over the curb and turned it violently around.

By now Reuben had started to gather his

thoughts, and he turned to Alma and smiled at her expression, flushed with excitement. "But, what are you going on about?" he grinned. "Who is going to do what?"

Alma laughed back at him. "Oh, well, you'll see."

Reuben leaned forward and looked across her and over at Zed as the old van tore through the city streets. But Zed only smiled back enigmatically. Moments later they pulled up to one of the condemned tower blocks. Zed bumped the van up onto the grass verge and they climbed out into the cold night air, the sound of sirens interweaving across the city.

"Come on," Alma shouted as she disappeared into the cavernous entrance. Zed looked at Reuben and shrugged. They followed her up the concrete stairwell, where the metallic smell of junk mixed with the tang of fresh urine, their way guided by a flickering strip of light on the fifth floor. Dance music flooded the hallway from an open door on one of the landings above them, and then the aromatic smell of skunk weed softened the acidic odors of the staircase. As they walked into the abandoned flat and sat down among the cushions and ashtrays, Reuben remembered Alma telling him about these squats; unoccupied buildings across the city which had been taken over by squatters who lived outside the system.

"Hi, you must be Reuben." A tall Rastafarian reached out to shake Reuben's hand through the smoke. Reuben nodded with a smile. "I'm Vincent. Your lady friend has told us all about the situation." He gestured towards Alma with his head. "We're ready."

But before Reuben could ask for more details, Vincent was already in conversation with someone else. And so he waited in suspense as his thoughts thickened and darkened like the smoke curling in the stale air. Reuben caught Alma's eye again and she smiled at him, and then turned back to the Japanese girl she had been talking to. A moment later, the girl stood up and turned to the room.

"Let's do this," she suddenly shouted at the assembled squatters. Vincent took a deep draught from the bottle of cider he had been holding, and then stood and slung a tattered rucksack over his shoulder. Within moments they were clattering down the stairway with shouts of excitement. Alma came up behind Reuben and grabbed his arm.

"You'll see, it all starts here," she whispered, squeezing hard. "The fucking revolution is beginning."

This time Alma drove with the Japanese girl and Vincent in the front. Reuben crouched against the rear door, holding onto the ply board cladding to steady himself as the van tipped against the force of Alma's turns, the wheels squealing on the damp tarmac. One of the squatters had brought a stereo, and techno pulsed from it as they raced across the city. Reuben looked at Zed, who sat in the opposite corner of the van hunched over his laptop, his blue-lit face creased in concentration. Finally they juddered to a stop and Alma pulled open the back door. Reuben started to climb out with the rest, but Alma touched his arm lightly to hold him back.

"Not you," she whispered as Reuben stepped back into the darkness.

"You okay?"

He turned, startled. He hadn't noticed that Zed had also stayed back. Reuben nodded and then climbed up over the front seats and looked out the window. He suddenly recognized the place. It was the substation they had visited a few days before. He could hear the squatters shouting now, and craned his neck to see Vincent spraying the word Anarchy across the front gate. A group of them had already cut their way through the razor wire and were in the courtyard. Then a tall blond kid pulled out a metal bar and started to smash the windows at the back of the building.

"What the hell are they doing?" Reuben asked quickly.

"Doesn't matter, just wait."

Zed turned back to the laptop as the wailing of sirens became audible over the shouts of the squatters. Within moments, blue light pierced the orange glow around the building. It was then that Reuben spotted the Japanese girl, crouching with Alma in the shadows. He watched as she kicked on a metal bar she had inserted along the edge of a doorway. As the flashing blue light reached their faces, they looked at each other like characters in a silent movie, and then they ran, leaving the door behind them slightly ajar.

Alma pulled the Japanese girl over the back wall just as the front gate burst open and fluorescent-jacketed policemen poured into the courtyard. Then Reuben felt movement behind him, and he turned to see Zed climbing into a set of blue overalls. For a moment the two men looked at each other without speaking, and then Zed pushed open the rear doors and stepped out. Without pausing, he strode up to the front gate, pulled a laminated identity card from his pocket, and nodded curtly at a policeman standing there. The policeman nodded back and then stepped aside, and Zed entered the facility, his laptop clenched under his arm. He walked quickly over to the side door that the Japanese girl had opened for him and pushed into the building.

***

41

The door clicked shut behind him, enclosing him in darkness. Zed exhaled slowly and listened, straining for a second until he could pick out the hum of a computer server. Within moments he was crouching next to the flickering lights of the machine. He plugged his laptop straight in and began to unpack the program he had prepared and copy it across to the substation. As he worked, he heard the tap and click of a door being opened at the back of the building, followed by footsteps. He pulled back into the shadows as he counted down the remaining seconds.

"Five, four, three...."

Then it was done, and he tapped the program into action and leaned forward to unplug his laptop. But as he reached across he noticed the icons on his screen beginning to disappear one by one. Zed tore the computer free, but it seemed to have no effect. Then the screen went blank. He checked the small red LED on the front of the server, but it burned back at him, unblinking. The program had failed. He could hear voices now inside the facility, and he moved quickly through the shadows back towards the side door. After a moment he pushed out into the blue light and walked quickly across the courtyard, almost tripping in his haste. The policeman who had let him in was speaking into a mobile phone, but as he passed the officer looked up.

"Zedekiah? Zedekiah, hold on please."

Zed started to run, and out of the corner of his eye he saw the brake lights on the van flicker as it moved away into the night. He sprinted through the dappled sodium-yellow streetlight towards the sound of traffic on the main road. Footsteps followed him like the echoes of his pounding heart as he turned a corner and ran into the highway, the draft of air from a passing truck brushing against his face as he crossed the northbound lane. Another car roared past his head as his foot buckled against the pavement.

Then there was a flash of light. The pain cleared his mind for a second. Zed scrabbled to his feet again and pushed forward, the shouts from the policemen fainter now behind the sound of traffic. He turned into the first alleyway he came to and headed towards the dark end, where the wind funneled out into an empty lot. Then he pushed the wire fence back at the point where it met the wall of the last building and ran out into the darkness. He couldn't hear his pursuers anymore and he slowed to a brisk walk, exhausted but anxious to clear the open ground.

"How the hell did they know who I was?" The thought revolved in his mind as he strode nervously through the darkness. When he reached the far side of the clearing, he turned back towards the squat.

***

The dotted line of his future path would shortly rejoin Alma and Reuben's as they guided the van towards the tower block through the backstreets, anxious to avoid a roving stop and search. They weren't yet aware of it, but another dotted line was also inscribed in thick red pen on the paper napkin of the future. As she tore the creaking Transit around a blind corner, Alma intersected this invisible line with a screech and thud, a white face pressed against the windscreen for an instant before disappearing under the bonnet.

She had already hit the brakes and the wheels shrieked as the tarmac sheared into the motionless rubber. Alma and Reuben jumped out and pulled the limp figure from under the van. The man's breath seemed to gurgle as they held him on either side and turned to haul him backwards onto the metal floor. When they had closed the van doors, Alma offered him a drink from her bottle of water, and through the matted hair a pair of crazed black eyes stared back, grateful, and then softening as recognition passed between them.

"You," Theo whispered as they looked at each other in the darkness.

CHAPTER 6

The drunken days had all merged into one long night of loneliness and fear as Theo tramped the cold streets like a ghost, and it took some time for him to remember exactly who he was, lying silently on a tattered sofa, longing for the bitter taste of alcohol.

"What would make it do that?" Zed was sitting on an overturned crate, his back against the damp wallpaper. Alma turned from the window, the fire-red sunset catching against the paleness of her skin, and at that moment, when she looked at the others, she felt a sudden rush of excitement. "This is fucking important," she said. Even Theo looked around, surprised by the conviction in her voice. "Don't you see? The fact that they knew who you are, the fact that the virus didn't work, it means we're really onto

45

something. Like they are doing everything they can to stop us."

"That's one way of putting it," Reuben laughed. "The point is we're screwed…they know where we live. We've nowhere to go now but here." He gestured around the dilapidated flat, the walls covered in graffiti, thick ribbons of wallpaper falling onto the faded carpet. Vincent the Rastafarian had opened the new squat for them with a blackened crowbar, prizing the door in a puff of masonry dust.

"You gotta get a lock on here," he had said to Reuben as they stood on the threshold, the damp smell wafting over them. It was one story above Vincent and the others, and the sound of dance music was just audible along the hallway. Zed and Alma had pushed past them into the thick, still air. They'd almost carried Theo up the seven flights of stairs, one on each side of him step by painful step, and now they let him fall back on the sofa, clouds of dust billowing around him as he hit the cushions. That was where he stayed as the others busied themselves. Reuben fixed a lock onto the back of the door, navigating the tell-tale screw holes of other squatters before them, while Zed and the Japanese girl connected the flat to the main electricity cable in the hallway. It wasn't until much later that Alma and Zed turned their attention back to Theo, who had fallen in and out of sleep while the others had been talking.

"If we take him to hospital, they'll ask too many questions," Alma said while Zed shook Theo's shoulder gently.

"Are you all right? I mean, are you in pain or something?"

Theo looked blankly back at him, his thoughts still running through the dark streets mad with fear. Then, forcing himself into the present, he pulled himself up onto his elbow and beckoned to Alma. She leaned forward, holding her black hair away with one hand, wincing involuntarily from the stench of sweat and wine.

"I was listening to you talking earlier. You want to hit the power grid, right?" Alma nodded and tried to stand, but Theo gripped her narrow shoulder and pulled her towards him urgently. "I have what you're looking for," he whispered. Then he released her and raised his voice so the others could hear. "Bring me a computer and I'll give you what you want."

"It's okay, man," Zed said quietly. "There's nothing you can do, but thanks though."

Theo sat up abruptly, wincing with pain. He was nearly shouting now. "Bring me a computer, you —" He was cut short by a coughing fit, and as he hacked desperately, Alma looked across at Zed and frowned.

"Okay, sure, don't worry, you can use mine."

Zed got up to fetch the machine.

While he was gone, Alma and Theo looked at each other, both remembering the incident on the bridge. Without speaking, it seemed as if an understanding passed between them, a knowledge of their intersected destinies, and Alma smiled at Theo knowingly as Zed arrived with the computer.

Theo slowly pulled himself upright, the broken sofa cracking underneath him, and held the machine uncertainly in his swollen, shaking hands. He wasn't prepared for this; the specter of those mocking eyes that had chased him from the station into the recesses of the city now filled his mind with dread. He traced the ridge around the lid of the computer uncertainly, his movements hesitant as he felt the others watching him, silent now in the rising evening gloom. The darkening room was filled only with the faint drumbeat of techno from the squat downstairs, and the sound of rain that had started to fall against the window. Theo let the roughened edge of the screen slide under his fingers thoughtfully. As the slight undulations in the plastic passed over his skin, he slipped through time again, leaping blindly backwards onto the moving metro train, out of the clanging tunnels and into the suburbs where the atomized lives threw pale shafts of lounge-light into the dark streets, through the momentary intimacy of the late-night snack bar, and back into the pool of milky light cast across his desk. He saw the code as it unfurled into the night, and he remembered Roxana.

As he listened to her voice repeating the words he had read, his fingers tightened around the edges of the screen and he flipped it open. While he waited for the machine to flicker into life, Theo's eye traced the vague outline reflected back at him, but saw only his own bowed head and the uneven back of the old sofa outlined in grey shadows.

"Okay," he said finally, breathing deeply. "So you want to turn the power off, right?" The three others stood now around the faint pool of light cast by the laptop screen as Theo began to write.

"But, you can't do anything," Zed said again, smiling almost imperceptibly. "There's a firewall you'll never get past...that's why we went there in the first place."

Theo wasn't listening. His fingers moved over the keyboard with a faint clicking sound, and he stared intently at the text that rolled across his screen. Zed looked at Alma and Reuben, and the three of them exchanged smiles in the darkness of the dilapidated flat. The storm outside had picked up, and it felt as if the building were swaying slightly in the wind. Reuben reached down and placed his hand on Theo's bony shoulder for a moment.

"Listen, thanks for trying," he said. "It's really cool of you to help us."

Theo stopped typing and looked up at them. For a moment, they all stood around the dancing light that the scrolling characters threw up from the computer screen and said nothing, listening only to the storm raging around them, rattling the window frames and swirling through the corridors.

"Wait." Alma looked up across the room suddenly. "The music." They listened for the drumbeat, but it had stopped. Zed ran over to the window, knocking over the table as he pushed his way through the darkness.

"Fuck." It was all he could say as he looked out. The others scrambled to join him and they all stood, unable to speak. It was as if a black carpet was being drawn over the city, covering up the lights district by district. Finally regaining himself, Reuben turned to Theo, who had remained sitting, the computer still in his lap.

"What the hell have you done?" His voice cracked. "What have you done?" His words were all but drowned out by the storm, which by now was howling around the building. Then the door of the flat burst open and the Japanese girl stood there breathlessly.

"What the hell's going on?" she screamed over

the din.

Zed pointed to Theo. "He's done it," he shouted. "He's turned out the lights."

They were all shouting now as more of the squatters piled into the flat, taking deep swigs from bottles of cider and wine they had brought with them. Reuben had opened the window and was hanging out, bellowing into the darkness.

"You can't control us anymore," he screamed, rain pouring off his shoulders and down his face. "It's our time now." But in the confusion, nobody noticed how Theo sat and looked darkly at the floor in silence.

Chapter 7

Theo didn't say much in the days that followed, but found a nebulous peace as the world of the squat swirled around him. The others left him alone, quietly respectful of the darkness that seemed to gather around the sofa in the corner where he had made his home. He would join them at mealtimes, pulling up an overturned crate as Zed passed around steaming bowls of freshly discarded food gathered from the bins of nearby supermarkets. He would listen quietly as the others talked, his thoughts flitting between the conversations and the shadows that stalked the perimeter of his mind.

"The world is changing, and we are the only ones who know it," Zed said after one meal of hot pasta and tuna as he leaned back on a broken chair. "It's as if everyone is sleeping except for us." He gestured out at the glittering spread of night underneath them. It had taken several hours for the authorities to get the lights back on, and in the darkness they had partied, pouring out of the building with whoops and bellows, and dancing into the dumbfounded rain-wet streets, their shouts echoing from the glistening, silenced walls. But order was quickly restored, the system righted itself, and in a handful of news reports the following morning, officials blamed the outage on a power surge. The world moved on, unaware of the significance of the breach, except for the group of squatters huddled around a makeshift table at the top of a darkened apartment building, and the shadows that kept watch over the small flat.

The dampness of autumn had begun to give way to the crisp freeze of winter, and the fallen leaves crackled underfoot as Reuben and Theo made their way across the estate one afternoon in search of food, their breaths lingering like pondered thoughts on the sharp air. They'd maintained a comfortable silence since Theo had arrived, but Reuben was desperate to know how he'd been able to hack into the grid so easily, and now that they were alone he took his chance.

"You feel better?" He broke the silence tentatively, unsure of how Theo would react. The question seemed to hang between them as Theo wrenched himself into the present.

"Sure." The word formed itself and rolled out reluctantly into the cold air.

The task completed, Theo turned his thoughts back in on themselves, but Reuben was not satisfied. He waited, then threw another question across the space that stretched between them.

"You were lucky. It could have been a lot worse, don't you think?" This time Theo slowed, momentarily thrown by Reuben's persistence. He let the words sink into his mind, but they dissolved immediately in the treacle-black swirl of his distraction, and he continued to walk in silence, the arrhythmia of their footsteps clattering awkwardly between them as Reuben waited for an answer. Then, as they turned out of the estate and onto the street leading to the supermarket, Reuben blurted, "But how did you do it? I mean, how the hell did you get inside the system so easily?"

Theo stopped and turned towards Reuben, his black eyes slowly flickering into life as he hauled himself up through his introspection. "Man, I'm really sorry for...." He trailed off, waving his hand back towards the estate. "Well, you know. But...." Theo shot a glance over his shoulder and then up the street behind Reuben before continuing. "The thing is that they're watching us, following every move we make."

Reuben stepped back slightly and tried to meet Theo's diverted gaze. "Who do you mean?" he asked. "Who's watching us?"

"Well, your friend Zed said the police knew his name. How is that possible? It's been the same for me. Ever since I first used the code, I've been seeing...." He stopped again, distracted by the memory of the ghostly face he had seen staring back at him from the computer screen. As he waited, Reuben shifted the rucksack he was carrying and watched Theo standing there, head bowed, puffs of condensation curling around the hood of his jacket and evaporating in the cold air that hung in the open grassland along the edge of the estate. Theo forced the image back into a fold in his mind and looked up at Reuben, straining through his fear. "It's like there's something else," he said finally, as if it was explanation enough.

Reuben put his hand on Theo's shoulder and nodded. "I think I know what you mean," he replied uncertainly, and they walked on in silence.

When they reached the rear gate of the supermarket, Reuben pulled himself up onto a side wall and lowered his hand to help Theo up. Then he swung himself around and dropped into the service area behind the closed store, and began to root around inside the dumpsters that were racked up against the back wall.

"So why did you decide to help us?" Reuben made it sound like a casual question, the urgency in his voice cloaked by the metallic echo from inside the chamber. He turned and caught Theo's eye momentarily as he handed him a packet of discarded garlic bread, and as he did so he caught a glimpse of something he did not understand in the way Theo looked back at him. "What's happened to you?" Reuben said suddenly, turning around to face Theo and placing a hand on his shoulder.

Theo looked down and saw Roxana's eyes gazing out at him from inside his thoughts. He let the two dark orbs hold him, their blackness intertwining with his.

Reuben tightened his grip on Theo's shoulder. "What is it?"

Theo looked up again, his eyes flickering in recognition. "It's nothing. It's just that I used to love someone, but she won't see me anymore. It's all...." His voice trailed off.

"But man, what you did with the code, it's incredible," Reuben said, his hand still resting on Theo's shoulder. "Shit, the world is changing because of you, surely that means something?"

Theo smiled weakly and stuffed the garlic bread

into the bag. "Yeah, thanks," he said, and Reuben turned back into the dumpster and continued passing packages back to him. Later that evening, Reuben's words came back to Theo as he gazed out over the city, his stomach full and warm. He really was making a difference, and maybe Roxana would realize that he had been right after all. As he listened to the others talking behind him, he looked across the cityscape and out to the horizon in the direction of the coast, where he could almost picture her sleeping.

CHAPTER 8

Theo felt a sense of peace for the first time in over a month as the terraced gardens finally gave way to open countryside. That morning, in the slow-motion consciousness that followed sleep, he had imagined Roxana again, and this time he knew that he had to see her. He'd pulled his hood low over his head and made his way out into the screeching, flat white day. In the station he stole a sandwich and ate it hunched over his laptop, his fingers moving urgently across the keyboard as he made his preparations.

The journey passed faster than he had expected, and the sea air was cold and unyielding when he stepped off the train and onto the deserted coastal station. He shivered as he entered the silent streets and started to scan the sweeping gardens, looking for the vaguely remembered dark green gables of her parents' house. As Theo walked he dawdled, unconsciously savoring the delay, but it wasn't long until he found himself looking directly into the blankly familiar stare of the uncurtained windows, emotionless under a thin canopy of winter trees. The garden path was longer than he remembered, and he shivered again as he stepped into the shadow of the porch and pushed through the thick, nervous air. Then the feeling evaporated as the door swung backwards and Roxana appeared like the manifestation of an almost-forgotten dream, her hair golden in the framed light of the hallway. He luxuriated in the sudden, unexpected warmth as they looked at each other in silence for an elongated moment. Then, finally, her face hardened.

"Well, what do you want?" She threw the words aggressively out into the pale light of the winter morning, but Theo had seen her unguarded look and pressed on.

"I...I've...." He paused, searching in vain for the words he had rehearsed on the train. "I want to show you something," he said finally.

Roxana moved back to admit him into the house. They sat on either side of the kitchen table, his tension ebbing away in the undulating warmth of a freshly lit fire. It was suddenly hard to distinguish the present from the refracted emotions of the past that echoed between them. Theo had forgotten the fine detail of her beauty, the frankness of her eyes, the faint worry lines that had begun to form in the crease of her forehead, her easy, conspiratorial smile.

"It's really nice to see you," he said finally, the words only a faint reflection of the almost unbearable urge he had to reach out and touch her bare arm. But Roxana seemed to understand, and she nodded slowly, waiting for more. "It's…I mean, I know things were difficult…." He paused. "For me it's been…" He stopped, suddenly unable to face those moments. He looked at her as she waited across the table, and it seemed to him that she was hardening again, that she had expected something else. Flustered, Theo pulled the laptop from his bag and placed it awkwardly in front of him. "Have you got your phone?" Roxana got up to fetch it, her curiosity overcoming her annoyance. "Go and check a news website, any one," Theo said, as the software broke free from under his fingers and spread out across the Internet. Roxana fell silent for a moment as she sat again and typed into the phone. Then her face reddened and she dropped it onto the table.

"What's this? What the hell are you doing, Theo?"

He looked down the blush of her neck to the small screen lying oblique in front of her. He could just see the words he had dispatched bannered across the top of the website. *Roxana I love you.*

"But, don't you like it? All those late nights, they were worth it, don't you see?" Theo's voice rasped now, straining to contain the situation.

"Worth it. Fucking worth it." Roxana was standing, willing him towards the door.

"I know you lied. I saw your emails. I thought..."

Her face flushed darker. "Leave me alone, Theo." She gestured down the hallway.

Theo slammed his computer closed, anger drowning out his sadness, and paused by the table, about to speak, his finger lingering on the warm wood.

"Leave now, Theo, and don't come back."

The phrase followed him out through the cold suburb, along the grating streets, and uphill to the deserted station. They sank into the cauldron of his fury as the train rattled back towards the city, and in that dark fire he resolved to break the world that had betrayed him. By the time he reached the squat he had calmed, his sadness buried underneath the anger, and the anger buried underneath the plan that had formed in his mind. As he stepped into the living room, Reuben threw him a knowing look, but Theo avoided his eyes and took up his position on the settee. After he had composed himself for a moment,

Theo looked up, his eyes burning black.

"I think it's time." The others turned towards him, surprised by the sudden vehemence in his voice. "I'm ready. Let's bring the whole thing down." He had barely spoken since he arrived, and a grin broke out across Reuben's bearded face.

"Fucking yes." Reuben put down the book he had been reading and leaned back on his chair, turning towards the others. "We'll delete society and start again. No more debt, no more mortgages, nothing."

But for some reason the moment seemed unbearably heavy as Reuben's words lingered on the damp air. Zed stepped across to the balcony and pulled open the door, letting the sounds of the city into the small flat. In the corner, Theo looked away, the blackness in his eyes merging with the shadows that oozed gradually into the room as evening fell.

CHAPTER 9

Zed set to work in the pool of pale light that the two screens cast into the room, his dreadlocks throwing arachnidan shadows onto the peeling walls behind him. Through the online message boards, his words propagated away from the small squat and out into the continents beyond, the rhythm of his fingers against the plastic keyboard resonating across the network as a thousand others joined him, turning their numbers against the sheer glass and concrete of the financial institution.

Alma could almost hear the thundering onslaught as she stepped out of the torrential rain and into the velvet light of the boutiques that ran underneath the bank. She caught a sudden glimpse of herself in a cafe window and paused to straighten the uncomfortably angular business suit and compose herself. Beyond the imperfect mirror of the glass she suddenly noticed Theo sitting in the far corner, his face milky white under the hood of his coat, staring intently at a laptop screen. To Alma he seemed unreal, almost translucent in the interplay of light against the glass, as if he had been projected from another dimension. Theo sensed her watching him and looked up from the computer, and for an instant their eyes met through the glass. Then Alma turned away, her heart fluttering uncomfortably as she moved towards the bank, intent now on her task.

The luxury of the corporate foyer was a world away from the dampness of the squat, yet somehow, in the ordered rows of shaded yellow lights and the impersonal, composed smile of the clerk, it seemed colder, less hospitable. Alma forced a faint smile as she approached the desk, her fingers playing over the rounded top of the memory stick in her pocket, and bent forward to murmur her name. The room was quiet, oblivious to the storm that now raged outside as thousands of computer browsers did battle with the bank's servers. The uniformed woman picked up a telephone and whispered into the receiver, and then gestured for Alma to sit.

But Alma remained standing, holding her rigid smile like a mask as a tired-looking woman in a creased suit emerged from a door behind the counter and led her along an amber-walled corridor until they reached her cubicle. "What can we do for you?" The woman gestured for Alma to sit on the far side of a laminated desk, her face cracking into an over-worn smile. At first Alma smiled back, mirroring her as best she could. Then the smile dropped from Alma's face and she stood again, the chair falling over behind her.

"What can you do? You can fucking take this," Alma shouted, accentuating the obscenity as she pushed the desk over with her foot. The woman tried to catch herself on the sliding papers, gasping wordlessly as Alma reached across the upended table and slammed the memory stick into the front of the computer that now lay on its side on the floor, the screen tipped backwards. Then Alma ran, punching her elbow into the glass face of a fire alarm as she turned back towards the exit, leaving the software behind her to burrow its way into the bank's servers and open a doorway for Theo. The alarm rippled upwards through the concrete building, and people started pouring out of the stairwells and into the corridor. Within moments Alma found herself submerged, pressing her body against the velvety wallpaper as she tried to squeeze past them out into the lobby. But she could only wait, frustration pounding through her veins as she inched forwards.

***

In the recesses of the cafe opposite, Theo saw people pouring out of the bank and set to work, moving his fingers silently across the computer keyboard to release the software. Then he closed the lid and got up, almost invisible as he made his way back out to the street where Reuben sat behind the wheel of the Transit van. Theo clambered in, and the two men waited for Alma to emerge, the sound of police sirens bearing down on them over the city traffic. Then blue light pierced the slate grey afternoon as the first police car turned into the street.

"Shit." Reuben looked at Theo and then desperately back at the entrance to the underground walkway, but Alma was still not there. A second squad car appeared, and Reuben engaged the engine, easing the van away from the front of the bank. As soon as he was out of sight, he slammed his foot down on the accelerator and tore into the back streets, the wheels squealing against the road. But as they turned around the second corner, there was a sickening jolt. The impact threw the two men forward against the plastic dashboard as the van began to swerve across the road. Reuben pulled himself back upright and looked into the wing mirror. Behind them he could see a rusted Volvo as it rammed the back of the van again, its one working light burning faintly in the overcast afternoon.

Reuben swung them into the next corner and tried to catch sight of the driver as they turned, but the interior was black and impenetrable. Then, as they pulled back out into the straight, the car hit them again. This time the impact pushed the van over the curb and up against the concrete flank of a building with a shriek. Reuben tore at the wheel and tried to wrench them away as the flat panel of a brick wall rose up in front of the windscreen in slow motion. But the car hit them again and the van met the wall head on, the bulkhead collapsing into the concrete.

***

Time almost seemed to stop as Reuben and Theo rose up off their seats and collided with the glass panel overhead. In front of them the van cut into the wall and began to slide, carefully gouging out two deep grooves in the brickwork and listing gradually over towards the roadway. Reuben watched as tiny shards of brick broke off silently from the wall and formed interlocking patterns in the air as they spiraled away from the leading edge. Then the moment glided forward again with a tearing sound and the shattering of glass as the side of the van hit the tarmac and spun out across the damp carriageway.

CHAPTER 10

The deafening waves of the alarm suddenly subsided and Alma moved forward again. She was almost at the exit now, and she tried to force her way past the two men in front of her. As she pushed against them, she suddenly caught sight of a small tetrahedron of dark blue ahead. But it was too late. She attempted to stop, but she was already moving and she emerged from the mass of people to find herself standing directly in front of a row of police who had formed a cordon across the front of the bank. They beckoned to a girl next to her and she stepped forward quickly to be searched. Then, as Alma prepared herself, she noticed a man in a dark suit standing slightly behind the police line. He held a small device in his hand, and when he turned to look towards Alma she caught a glimpse of the photograph on the screen. It was her, taken as she'd followed the woman into the bank earlier that day.

A crease of recognition passed across the man's face as they looked at each other, but by the time he started shouting she was already moving backwards. Once she was several rows behind, Alma turned and ran, past the waiting people and back into the building. She tore open the first doorway she came to and stumbled into a chaotic office room, breathing hard. There was another door on the far side and she headed straight for it, scattering papers and bits of stationery as she pushed the desks aside. Then she was running along another, nearly identical corridor. But this time there was a stairway at the end, its white-painted walls leading directly upwards into the heart of the building. Alma paused at the bottom, taking stock for a moment. Then she heard voices enter the corridor behind her and she pulled herself into a small alcove underneath the lowest flight of stairs, drawing her knees out of sight against the rough underside of the concrete just as the men thundered past her and up into the building, throwing giant shadows onto the wall as they went.

Then there was silence, and Alma took her chance. She ran into the quiet space they had left behind, coiling upwards until she had to stop, blackness pulling at the edges of her mind while she struggled for breath. She was near the top by now, and as her clarity returned she realized that the doorway in front of her was different from the others, rich and dark. She pushed against it instinctively and stepped into the unexpected opulence of an executive suite. Painted faces looked down on her from the walls as she nudged aside an oxblood leather chair and slipped underneath the great table that filled the room. Alma flattened herself against the broad support at the end and pulled her knees up tight against her chin so she could cower there in the semi-darkness, dreams of pursuit and imprisonment mingling with the interlocking shadows as she slowly sank fetus-like into the thick pile carpet.

Sometime later a man's voice reached into her jumbled thoughts and pulled her awake, and for a long while she lay motionless, watching the gleaming black shoes as they made their way around the edge of the table, her mind struggling to reconstruct the sequence of events that had led her there.

"No, no that's right." She could only hear a slight crackle in the phone speaker as the other person replied. "We're lucky it didn't come from within the system, totally yes." The man's voice was rich, almost creamy. Alma tried not to breathe as the feet stopped right next to her and turned outwards. Then the wood above her head creaked and groaned as he pulled himself up onto the table edge, his feet swinging dangerously close. "Apparently a woman." The man shifted his weight above her. "Yes."

Then he released a long peal of nasal laughter, and underneath him Alma shivered.

CHAPTER 11

Reuben opened his eyes and blinked, trying to focus on the vertical plastic of the upended dashboard. He reached down to free the seatbelt, peeling it slowly away from the warm blood that was seeping along the side of his body, and looked across at Theo, who was slumped sideways, his face white and motionless, his eyes glazed with shock. Gritting his teeth through the pain, Reuben wrenched his arm across his body and turned to release Theo's seatbelt. Theo fell forwards onto Reuben's legs, and as Reuben lay motionless, crushed by pain, he suddenly noticed shadows moving across the mottled plastic in front of him. He traced the movement backwards, up through the smashed window to where two figures stood looking over the broken windscreen, their faces hooded and obscured. The shadow passed across Theo and he stiffened, suddenly cold as one of them craned over the front of the van, filling the cabin with the flat, peppery smell of death. Reuben held his breath and waited while they looked at him and Theo for a long moment. Then the shadow lifted and they silently withdrew. Reuben watched the unbroken sunlight until he was sure they had gone, and then he grasped Theo's damp black hair and shook his head urgently.

"Come on." His voice cracked with the effort. "We need to leave." Theo looked back at him unblinkingly. "Theo, we need to get out," Reuben said again. Theo nodded silently, and then grimaced with effort as he rolled forwards out of the seat so that his back was up against the shattered pane of the windscreen, which still hung loosely from its frame. The weight of his body was enough to push a hole through the glass, and Theo fell forwards awkwardly onto the road. Reuben followed, pulling himself over the dashboard and onto the tarmac. Then he tried to stand among the scattered glass and metal, but his leg buckled underneath him with the effort, blood oozing down the inside of his trouser leg. Theo pulled him up again and held onto his shaking arm as the two men limped slowly away from the wreckage.

***

Night was falling, and they shuffled slowly, dipping in and out of the shadows. Every few minutes Reuben would stop, lowering himself roughly onto the pavement, his back bent awkwardly to one side as he tried to keep his injured leg off the ground. They didn't speak much, each occupied with his own private fear.

Reuben struggled to stay awake, the tearing pain overwriting his consciousness at each step, while beside him another type of darkness leeched into Theo's mind. The same fear that had sent him running out into the derelict city so many days before haunted him now as they walked across the threshold into night. In the darkness, his thoughts turned back to the strange figures who had stood over them and filled the crumpled van with the stench of death. For some reason he knew that they were connected to the face that had leered at him from behind his darkened computer screen so many nights ago. It was as if it had broken through the membrane that demarks the limits of the digital world, and he began to keep a nervous watch on the gathering shadows that followed them.

They had been moving forward in this way for several hours before he saw it. He had lowered Reuben to the ground again, pausing to catch his breath, when he caught a movement, a slight distortion on the edge of his vision. Theo turned towards the shadows at the end of the street, his quickened breath sending thin grey plumes of water vapor into the column of streetlight as he scrutinized the darkness. Then he saw it deform and bend as if someone was lurking there.

"Them," he whispered to himself. Reuben looked up from his own tunnel of fear.

"Who?" Theo didn't hear the question at first, his mind turned in on itself. "What's up?" Reuben's voice seemed remote, disembodied, as Theo crouched close to the wall watching the darkness, trying to force his eyes to pierce the shadows.

"Shit, I don't know," he said finally. "Maybe I'm just losing it." Both men stopped and watched the motionless street. After a while a cat jumped out of one of the gardens and sat on the sodium yellow pavement looking back at them.

"I can't see anything," Reuben said finally, and Theo shrugged and hoisted Reuben up again, before turning back along the tunnel of streetlamps. By now they were just a few streets from the squat and they quickened their pace, but as they turned through the sleeping houses Theo could not stop looking back at the shadows moving behind them. Then, as he got ready to haul Reuben back to his feet again after one of their pauses, he suddenly froze. A dark figure peeled away from one of the shadows to cross a driveway, the torso clearly visible in the yellow light. Theo nudged Reuben.

"Stand up slowly," he whispered, "but look over there." Reuben shifted his arm across Theo's back, and as he did so shot a glance back down the street.

"Wait," Reuben said, pausing. "We're leading them right back to Zed." They stopped, suddenly uncertain. Reuben eased himself back down again, grimacing. "Anyway, I can't do this much longer." The words came involuntarily through the pain. Theo looked back down the street, but the figure had pulled into the shadow again. So they waited, the cold night creeping into their clothes as the darkness lay still.

After a while Theo nudged Reuben. "What should we do?" But Reuben didn't reply. "Man...." Theo nudged him again. Then he looked across at Reuben's bowed head and saw that his eyes had closed. "Shit." Theo crouched in front of Reuben and reached around his body to lift him, but then he pulled away. Reuben's left side was sticky with blood. Theo tried to pull him to his feet, straining against the deadweight, and as he did so Reuben sighed, his eyes half opening.

"I'm tired, let me sleep here for a bit."

"Come on, we need to go." Theo's voice was dry

with exhaustion, and he pushed his shoulder against Reuben's arm and pulled him upwards. The two men continued their slow, painful journey across the forecourt of the estate, while the shadows gathered and dispersed silently behind them.

The building cast a pale yellow glow out onto the concrete, and as they stepped towards the pool of light Theo noticed a hooded figure just visible under an alcove at the edge of the hallway. The head turned towards them slowly as they approached, and for a moment Reuben and Theo looked straight into the blackness where the face should be. Then, as if a silent conversation had taken place, the dark figure suddenly bowed its head and hurried past them, away from the building and out into the darkness of the estate.

Reuben and Theo pushed on through their exhaustion, winding up the acrid staircase back to the squat. But as they stepped out onto the landing they paused again. The door of the flat hung unnaturally open, bent back on its hinges. Theo lowered Reuben against the concrete wall, grunting with the effort, and walked up to the opening.

"Zed," he whispered into the doorway, but no reply came. He pulled the door back carefully and stepped into the darkened apartment. At the end of the hallway cream-colored light spilled out onto the carpet, and as Theo reached it and turned into the dim glare of the computer screens, he saw the back of Zed's head silhouetted against the light.

"Zed." Theo stepped forward and put his hand on Zed's shoulder. The weight caused Zed's chair to slowly turn on its axle, sending the spider-shadows scuttling across the wall. And then Theo fell back, gasping at the horror as Zed's dead, frozen face screamed back at him silently in the half-light.

CHAPTER 12

The silent scream followed him as he ran out into the fluorescent hallway. It echoed from the concrete walls and drowned out his panic as he dragged Reuben away from the broken door of the flat. It made the air pulse against his cold, damp skin as he pushed himself against the far wall and buried his head in his knees. Theo seemed to lose hold of time as he sat there, rocking slightly against the painted wall. He wasn't sure if he slept, or if his thoughts had just stayed hidden in the recesses of his mind, but in the unwelcome blackness nightmares shuffled by, causing the air to waft across Theo's face as he cowed against the unyielding concrete.

The shrill, discordant hum of his terror resonated through the other space that connects us, its off-key harmonies passing across the concrete and metal world of molecules, its ancient language unhindered in the darkness until it blended with another, sweeter tone, the spinning thoughts of Alma as she too drifted along the boundary of consciousness, curled in fear in a darkened office block.

***

She wasn't aware of it, but the signal roused her, blinking and listening to the hiss of silence that now filled the empty room. Alma winced as she flattened her legs against the thick carpet. She had been locked in the same curled position for hours, and painful pockets of acid had begun to clump in her muscles. She grasped the edge of the table and pulled herself slowly upright as if she was dragging her semi-conscious body from a pool of dark water, and then she stood against the window, the city glistening below her. Its distant lights danced across her face as her breath condensed against the glass, while Theo's urgent harmonies still resonated underneath her slowly forming thoughts.

Theo also dreamed of light. Narrow shafts of red that strafed the walls of the darkened, concrete hallway, reflected from the door of the open flat as if a digital fire was burning there. A sense of sudden urgency made Alma turn away from the window, and in his fear-soaked darkness, Theo turned away also, pushing his face into the cold ridges of concrete as the red web of light filled the air.

Alma made it to the stairwell, anxious to flee the building. She stood for a moment, running her hand absent-mindedly against the cold walls, her fingers playing on the ridges between the bricks as her consciousness crystallized and hardened. Then she ran, spiraling dizzyingly downwards through the fluorescent tunnel, her feet almost slipping on the steps. At the bottom she paused momentarily, her hands resting across the metal bar of a fire door as she caught her breath, and then she sunk the latch and burst out into the cold night air, an alarm erupting behind her as the building registered the breach, its shrieking accusation echoing through the empty hallways. Theo stirred, as if he could almost hear the beating of Alma's feet as she ran out into the dark streets behind the building, winding her way towards the squat, before he slipped back into the terrifying dream world as the sound of scratching and scraping filled the blackness around him.

***

"Wake up, Theo," Alma whispered, so close that her musky smell enveloped him. Theo sat up slowly, her voice finally pulling him from the darkness of his dream into the flat, grey dawn. The door of the apartment was lying across the hallway as if it had been flung violently aside during the night. Theo looked up at her, and then raised a shaking arm and pointed to the sheared doorframe, his mouth dry and wordless. He turned to Reuben, who hadn't moved since Theo had dragged him against the wall earlier that night. Alma climbed over him and knelt down to hold his head in her hands. At first Reuben did not respond. But after Alma held him for a few minutes, talking softly, he finally blinked and opened his bloodshot eyes, looking from one to the other. Alma smiled with relief and pulled him to his feet.

Once Reuben was standing, supporting himself against the wall, she began to walk him slowly towards the open doorway of the flat, but Theo reached out and grabbed her sleeve, struggling to speak.

"Wait," he whispered finally, but Alma had already pulled away and shook her head as she carried Reuben slowly up to the threshold.

"We need to get him inside," she said. Theo pulled her back desperately.

"We can't go in there. Zed...." He trailed off, unable to shake the horror from his mind.

"Zed what?"

Theo pointed to the door again, "Zed...."

But she had already left Reuben leaning against the concrete wall and stepped through the doorway and into the flat. Theo followed her back inside, the stench of death still hanging from the torn wallpaper. But then he stopped in shock as he looked into the room at Zed's empty chair, which seemed to turn imperceptibly in front of two smashed computer screens.

"But, he...."

Alma stepped wordlessly outside again and helped Reuben, leading him slowly to the same settee which had been home to Theo just the day before. Theo walked back to the door in his confusion and looked into the hallway, to where Reuben's blood smudged the concrete floor. Then he noticed another red line merging with the blood. It was paint from a graffitied image on the wall. Theo followed it upwards and looked in horror at the grimace of a blood-red face that leered down over the place where they had slept.

CHAPTER 13

They upended the table against the open doorway and then closed their eyes against the flat light of day. Alma lay face down on an old mattress with her arm slung around the top of Reuben's head, while Theo curled against the wall, his coat rolled under his neck. There they slept until the light began to fade again, turning the room deep sunset-red. When they awoke, Reuben's blood had spread across the mattress, and Alma tore strips from the sheet and dressed the wound as best she could while he lay gulping through the pain. Then, before the darkness came, they left the squat for good, inching down the stairwell step by painful step. The lights in the building were out permanently now, and darkness dripped slowly over the concrete until it submerged them completely.

When they finally stepped out into the chaotic night, the air was filled with wood smoke and distant voices. But it wasn't until they had made their way out of the estate that Theo noticed the others, lingering on the edges of shadows that pooled between the street lights. In the windows of the darkened shopfronts he caught glimpses of them, darting forward, their faces obscured. Theo waited until he entered the warm light of the underground station before looking back, out along the tiled entranceway and into the pregnant darkness beyond, to where the shadows bulged and distorted.

The three of them cut an unusual image as they loitered for the train, dark clad and unwashed, their eyes furtive. Reuben was standing unaided now, but his face was deathly pale, his lips cracked and washed out. Earlier that evening Alma had told them of an apartment, an empty attic across the city where they could hide for a while. It had almost been hers once, but the deal had fallen through, the developer gone bankrupt, and so it remained half-finished, half-bought.

"We'll be safe there," she'd said as they stood on the balcony of the squat looking out over the city for the last time. "No one will find us."

As the train pulled away, blurring the world

outside into ochre and gold, she leaned up against the curved glass wall of the carriage and smiled to herself, half closing her eyes. Reuben too had stretched across two facing seats and appeared to be sleeping.

But opposite them, Theo sat forward, his eyes moving wildly up and down the carriage as the train thundered through the darkness. He had just begun to relax too, lulled by the rhythmic undulations of the train, when a shift in the light at the far end caught his attention. He looked up at the stained Perspex that divided one carriage from another, directly into the black pools of two dark eyes that watched him through the window. The features were indistinct, but the look was unmistakable.

Theo stood in shock, wild-eyed, as he gripped one of the yellow plastic poles for support. Then, in the shriek of the slowing train he stumbled forward, his eyes glistening with sudden fear.

"What the hell?" Alma grabbed his arm.

"We need to get off the train." His voice was rasping and dry, and it took Alma a few moments to understand him. By now Reuben was standing too, and he looked at Alma uncertainly. Theo was already at the doorway, and as the train slowed he turned to Reuben. "It's been watching us the whole way." Theo moved his head in the direction of the small window, and Reuben followed the movement and looked at the plastic door, but the window was empty now.

"Who? Who's been watching us?"

"In the other carriage," Theo shouted back over the sound of the opening doors.

"What on earth was that all about?" Reuben asked again as the train was sucked back into the tunnel and they were left on the almost-empty platform.

"It was following us." Theo looked around them wildly. "It was one of them, I know it." He craned his neck to look along the pillars that ran the full length of the station, but no one emerged. Reuben and Alma glanced at each other, then Reuben walked over and rested his hand on Theo's shoulder.

"Are you okay? I didn't see anything."

But at that moment the air sheared as another train bore down on the station, and Theo didn't respond. They boarded again and continued the journey in silence, Reuben and Alma both lost in their own worlds, Theo keeping watch nervously on the small window at the end of the carriage.

The apartment was on the other side of the city and the stations passed quickly, small islands of yellow light in the darkness. By the time they got off and emerged at street level, cold rain had started to fall. The building was just behind the station, its glistening concrete walls cloaked in scaffolding, its windows lachrymose in the darkness as they kept watch over the empty street.

"Hold on," Alma said as she swung herself up onto the wooden platform and disappeared into the darkness. Moments later the front door opened and she let them in. The apartment was empty, wires looping their way across the bare walls, blue plastic sheeting still hanging from the newly fitted window panes. A pot of white paint had spilled across the floor in front of the door and caked dry. Reuben pulled over a small step and winced with pain as he sat, while Alma clattered about in the kitchen. All the while Theo kept watch over the street below, leaning against the unpainted window frame as they ate cold tinned spaghetti.

After the meal, Reuben and Alma went into the back room and lay on the bare mattress in silence. Theo was about to give up too and turn back into the shadows when he caught a movement. As he scrutinized the small patch of black, he could just make out a figure standing there in the darkness.

CHAPTER 14

Razer spun the cold stem between his fingers and tried again, leaning in close this time, his face almost touching her hair. "What are you drinking, sweetheart?" His voice sounded salacious, the vowel sounds dripping off his tongue like globules of saliva. This time the redhead was annoyed.

"Just fuck off, all right?"

He stepped back, steadying himself on the bar, and straightened the lapels of his pinstripe thoughtfully. Then he smiled to himself, tipped the rest of his frosted glass back with a flourish, and slammed it down onto the bar. He turned in towards the maze of tables, his eyes fixed decisively on the copper curve of the bathroom door handle on the far side.

It took longer than he had expected for it to come within reach, and Razer grasped it with relief, steadying himself for a moment before plunging the latch and pushing the door open. Once inside he stepped into a stall and began to rummage through his wallet, cards and crumpled receipts falling around him like dead leaves until his fingers closed in on the small plastic bag. Razer held the half-gram of grey-white powder up to the light, forcing his eyes to focus on it. Then he started to scoop it clumsily into his nostril with the inside nail of his little finger, grunting with the effort. When he had finished it off, he sat back on the toilet seat and eyed the debris scattered around him while his face began to flush. Then he stuffed the cards back into his jacket pocket, kicked the door open, and stumbled out of the bar.

As he stepped into the cool night air Razer breathed deeply, taking in lungfuls of the pungent city as the light breeze swept back his thinning blond hair. A feeling of satisfaction fell over him as he walked slowly through the midweek crowd, the sound of chatter ebbing in and out of earshot. Then, suddenly doubling back, he turned towards one of the clubs, the music giving him a tingling sensation as it washed over him.

"White Russian," he drawled at the bored brunette behind the bar. While she worked, Razer searched through the debris in his jacket pockets, and then pulled out a gold credit card and pushed it across the bar in front of him. After a moment, the woman turned back, dour with irritation.

"I'm sorry, it's been declined."

"For God's sake," Razer said, and pulled out a handful of cards from the suit jacket pocket and selected another. He tossed it over to her without looking up, but after a moment she turned back to where he leaned against the bar.

"I'm sorry," she said again, her voice shrill with irritation. Razer pulled the stack of cards out, and as he began to rifle through them someone fell against him, scattering them on the floor.

"Bloody idiot." He swiveled angrily, but they had already disappeared back into the crowd. Razer scrabbled around on the floor to gather them up and stood again, swaying slightly as he handed another one to the bartender. The machine refused it again and she returned it to him without speaking. Razer slammed his fist against the plastic bar top. "Oh come on," he shouted, furious, handing her another card.

The woman shook her head this time. "Maybe you should go home."

"Who the hell do you think you are?" Razer was shouting now, and people began to look around as his fury rose above the music. Then he reached forward to get the drink, and as he did so he knocked over an ice bowl, sending the cubes rattling over rows of bottles stacked behind the bar and out onto the floor. The woman gestured to someone out of sight, and a moment later a thick hand rested on Razor's wrist and forced the drink back onto the bar.

"You're going to leave now." A heavy, eastern European voice accentuated the last word menacingly as the man pulled Razer backwards across the dancefloor. Then Razer was outside, sitting, surprised, on the damp pavement in front of the entryway. "Don't come back," the security man said, his accent making the words sound like a death threat.

Razer stood and raised his middle finger drunkenly to the man's back before stumbling towards his flat, muttering to himself as he went. On his way back, he tried to buy a bottle of wine before he remembered that he didn't have any cash. As he stepped out into the night again, the man called him back.

"You dropped something," a fat hand gestured over the counter. It took a few moments for Razer to notice the paper napkin that had fallen onto the floor, and he picked it up, thanking the man with an annoyed nod. Razer was just about to toss it when he noticed a mark across the surface. He unfolded it and read the message out loud.

Razer – meet me tomorrow evening in the park opposite your flat.

He stuffed the napkin back into his shirt pocket with a baffled frown as he ambled away.

That was the last thing he remembered about that night, and as soon as he awoke in the early afternoon he pulled his shirt up onto the bed and reread the note as he lay there, his head spinning.

CHAPTER 15

The park gate stood out, even among the smart buildings of the expensive West End neighborhood, its Victorian over exuberance incongruous against the limp saplings and roughly painted railings. Reuben leaned back onto the crumbling bark of an old elm tree, his body stiff with pain, and waited. He knew Razer would come. It was in his nature to be confrontational, and he didn't have anything to lose. They had been unlikely friends, Razer and him. Razer was the kind of person that Reuben normally hated for his air of privileged entitlement. He was expensively educated and always treated like an insider. But they had struck an instant friendship anyway, drawn together by a shared indifference, and something deeper...a sense of unease about the system that controlled them.

Reuben's thoughts suddenly dispersed as a hand grasped his shoulder, and he looked up into Razor's eyes, which were already narrowed against the stark blue late-afternoon light. The two old friends smiled at each other, and then Razer stepped back, the smile quickly fading from his creased face as he looked up and down Reuben's tattered clothing.

"What on earth's happened to you?" he drawled. "You look like a tramp." Reuben flushed for a moment, suddenly feeling ridiculous. But then he remembered Zed, and Theo's dark warnings, and glanced nervously behind Razer at the sparse shrub line and empty streets.

***

Razer frowned as he watched Reuben shoot suspicious looks around him like a lunatic. Life had been cruel to Razer. From an early age he'd assumed a practiced smile under which he could bury his doubt. He had always followed the rules, joined the right clubs, and played the right sports. He had been rewarded for his acquiescence at first. He got a job managing an investment fund, and made money by doing nothing but following the advice of well-paid underlings. But it was as if the system somehow knew he was a fraud, and one day it turned sour. He started losing money as the markets moved against him time after time, until eventually the management had taken him quietly aside. He took up an administrative job, but it barely paid the rent, and pound by pound his money had dwindled into debts.

As the two men looked at each other, the light around them crossed the ridge that divided day from evening and began its gradual descent into night. Reuben leaned in close, his voice dropping to a whisper as if he feared someone might overhear.

"Listen, we're going to fuck the system, erase everything, and set the world free." Razer caught a slight smell of sawdust and plaster on his friend as the shadows gathered around them. "But we need your help." The tree branches overhead began to creak indiscreetly in a sudden gust of wind as Reuben spoke, and he stepped right next to Razer, placing a hand on his shoulder. "We need someone on the inside."

Razer nodded, his eyes glittering at the idea as the two men walked slowly through the darkening park to discuss their plan. Reuben told him about Theo, the hacker who could get past any firewall, about Alma and what she had heard as she cowered hidden in the stricken bank. Every now and then Razer nodded as night gradually rose around them. They needed someone on the inside, someone who could access the central clearing network and help them insert the code into the heart of the system. As Reuben talked, Razer was sizing up the risk. He hated the system that had given him everything and then taken it all away, but he wasn't stupid. Reuben hadn't said anything in particular, but somehow Razer sensed there was more.

"Why all the secrecy? Why couldn't we have just met for lunch?"

They walked in silence for a moment, listening to the stiff wind as it stirred the late autumn leaves, then after a deep breath Reuben continued.

"It's just that...." He hesitated, unsure where to start. "It's...we are being followed."

Razer nodded. "Okay, we need to be careful, I understand," he said finally.

CHAPTER 16

As autumn yielded gradually to winter, Razer ran his mind back and forth over the question. He repeated it in his thoughts, during his flat grey commute, through the solitary lunches and as he tipped his glass to the unfriendly night, until one morning he decided to act. Reuben had been careful, careful enough that the hollow eyes which shadowed him as he moved across the city hadn't cast their pall over Razer. Careful enough that the two men had agreed on a code, and like a character from a spy novel, Razer signaled his decision by leaving a curtain drawn all day. Later that evening they met again, standing side-by-side like strangers in a city bar.

"What took you so damn long?" The wait had

taken its toll on Reuben, and he had grown irritable. Razer was caught off-guard by the unexpected directness of the question, and he took a couple of lingering mouthfuls of wine before answering.

"You've got no idea what you're asking for, have you?" His drawl seemed to coil snakelike around Reuben's exposed neck. "They're gonna burn me if this doesn't work, and they'll burn you too, you stupid twat." The obscenity made them both splutter with muted laughter, and Reuben looked quickly across at his friend and smiled.

"I have an appointment next month, I'll do it then," Razer said after another long mouthful. "It's at a clearing house. They keep tally on all the day's transactions. They hold the supply of money that props the whole system up."

"Shit, mate, that'll do it for sure," Reuben said as Razer flashed him another smile. Reuben stood quickly and grinned back, then he turned and stepped out into the evening mist, letting a small piece of paper spiral to the floor behind him. Razor's well-manicured hand plucked it from the air at the exact instant it touched the concrete floor, folded it in a precise square, and slipped it into an inside pocket. He finished his drink slowly, savoring the moment. It was the first time he had felt anything other than disillusionment for longer than he cared to remember.

Over the next few weeks, Razer diligently committed the code to memory. He clipped it to his fridge with a magnet depicting the Eiffel Tower, and by the time he was ready for his trip he could write it out in full. He was still muttering it to himself when he took a taxi to the airport, and while he worked his way through a plate of free sandwiches in the business lounge he wrote it out again on the back of a paper napkin. As the small aircraft accelerated into the murky sky, pulling him back reassuringly into the leather seat, he finally let the symbols slip out of his thoughts. The undulating whine of the Rolls Royce engines pulled him further, away from the plastic-clad cabin and into the dark world of his dreams, where he circled a great black pit. Every now and then he tried unsuccessfully to throw himself in as the aircraft fell abruptly in air turbulence. Razer strained deeper and deeper into the blackness until he was suddenly pulled headlong. As he fell, two interlocking swirls of light appeared like ancient galaxies, and then the image was gone in a crash of light as the plane dropped heavily onto the tarmac and the metallic voice on the intercom announced their arrival. Razer looked around and felt as if the other passengers had been watching him as he slept.

He made his way quickly through town, nervous

now as he crossed the ravine and entered the financial district, its buildings understated, set discretely back from the road amid blank, manicured lawns. The taxi swept up one of the driveways and crunched to a halt outside an anonymous building. As he stepped out of the car, Razer tried to smile at the driver, but his coda was unnatural, overemphasized, and the dark-eyed man looked away quickly as if sensing something amiss. Razer hesitated in front of the concrete and glass panels, loitering among his reflections as he straightened his tie and tried to put the misstep out of his mind. Then another man's image formed beyond the reflections, and with a flick of his hand Razer swept the images away, sending the automated doors reeling backwards with a series of clicks, and stepped into the building.

The sallow, greying man greeted Razer with an absent-minded handshake, and led him down a fluorescent passageway into the building. As they walked past rows of unmarked doors, Razer marveled at how bland it was. It handled some of the biggest financial transactions in the world, processing billions for governments and banks, yet it was as featureless as a rented office. The man led him into a windowless meeting room, where almost identical men and women sat waiting for him, and Razer delivered his presentation on autopilot, barely aware of the blank faces that looked on. As the words spilled out of his mouth, Razer noticed a terminal in the corner of the room. Reuben had told him that all he needed to do was enter the code into the computer to disable its defenses, and then download the software from the Internet and set it to work. Once he had finished, his audience asked a few polite questions and then stepped out into the hallway. Razer turned to his host and spoke the phrase he had been practicing, making it sound as natural as possible.

"Sorry, my phone's not working. Can I just check my mail?" The words sounded artificial, rehearsed, and Razer winced as he heard them and prepared for the greying man in front of him to refuse. But he simply nodded and leaned over to enter his password before letting Razer sit. Then the man followed his colleagues out into the corridor, and as they spoke in muffled voices Razer sat in the corner of the meeting room and began to work, his fingers shaking as he downloaded the software, and then brought up a command prompt so he could write out the code that Reuben had given him.

Once his colleagues had dispersed, the man came back into the room and waited impatiently in the doorway, his face obscured by shadow. Razer read over the code one last time to make sure he hadn't got anything wrong, and then stood and forced another smile as he activated it, and then released the software he had downloaded into the network.

CHAPTER 17

Three hundred miles away, Theo got ready for the signal. They had been in the flat for weeks, eating takeaways on the floor, or off a tattered coffee table Reuben had found out in the street, its wood-effect plastic laminate frayed and peeling with damp. In the first few days Alma had hung some fabrics up over the windows, bathing the interior in patterned orange light. Theo sat now along the seam between two shifting, interlocking patterns, his back against the wall. The computer was open in front of him on the floor as he waited for a sign that Razer had been successful. There were no interior doors, but Reuben and Alma had made the back room theirs, pinning a sheet across the bare lintel, their clothing forming damp piles around an old mattress, while Theo had been sleeping on a bed made of unfolded cardboard boxes in the corner of the main room. Across the unvarnished floorboards, the misshapen disks of dead candles marked out the long, uncomfortable nights as they had waited on Razer.

Reuben's silhouette craned forward against the shafts of orange light, his movement sending a cosmos of suspended dust spinning like galactic vortices out into the center of the room, and pulled back the edge of the hanging material to look down on the intersection below. Ever since they had arrived, someone had always been standing there in the shadows, watching, waiting. They were easy to spot, each one different but always the same, their faces obscured by a hooded sweatshirt or a baseball cap, their attention averted as if they were pretending not to look. Once Reuben had gone down to confront one of them, a tall, skinny figure in a grey hooded top and tattered trainers, but he had hurried away without speaking, head bowed, only to return minutes later. The one standing there now suddenly looked up, turning the black space where his face should be towards the window. Reuben felt a sudden tingle along his spine as he looked back into the small patch of darkness, and he let the fabric fall back across the pane, dissolving the shard of yellow sunlight that had transected the room for a moment.

Then it happened. Theo shouted out quickly. Reuben and Alma crouched next to him against the plasterboard, their faces pale and distant in the blue light of the screen. They had waited for so long that they had almost forgotten what it felt like, the cold sharp edge of excitement now cutting through them as they lingered on the edge of the precipice, the relentless blinking of the cursor like a battle drum. The code that Razer had implanted would notify them once it was active by making a deposit of one dollar into Theo's bank account. To activate it, all Theo had to do was to transfer the dollar back, and the code would begin its work, deleting the records that enabled the financial system to function, wiping the slate clean, and pressing the reset button on society. Theo looked at Reuben and then at Alma, suddenly nauseous with vertigo.

"Let's do this," Reuben whispered.

But as Theo reached forward to the keyboard to begin the transfer, the front door imploded, sending thick splinters of wood spiraling out into the room. Behind it a man stood on the threshold, swirls of wood dust momentarily radiating from his bowed head, his face obscured underneath a baseball cap. Reuben scrambled to his feet and leapt forwards towards the door with a shout, but before he could get there the man raised his head, his eyes gaping black, and opened his mouth.

His silent scream threw Reuben backwards with its force. Theo tried to type, but the computer slipped from his fingers in the howling wind and smashed against the far wall. Outside the windows had turned black as if a vast storm was raging overhead. Theo looked across at Alma, who had grabbed onto a loose cable and was now hanging from it as the wind pulled her backwards, her face a blur in the sudden darkness. He thought he saw her shouting, but he could not hear it. There was a flash of pain, and then nothing.

CHAPTER 18

When he awoke, Reuben lay for a while against the wall, his tongue lingering over the taste of blood. The room was dark and silent, and he winced with pain as he pulled himself upright. He couldn't see the others anymore and he called out, but his voice died away quickly, absorbed by the torn, damp walls of the flat. From outside, shades of mottled green light shifted against the surface of the window. Reuben made his way towards it, dragging himself slowly down the stairwell and out to the street, his movements strained and heavy as if he was underwater. Then he began to panic as he looked around the deserted roadway. He circled, confused, terrified, eventually grabbing a lamp post as the bitter taste of nausea welled up in his throat. Reuben leaned against the metal for a moment, seeking reassurance from its familiar coldness, and looked upwards at the swirling clouds that bubbled above him like the surface of a boiling liquid.

***

Alma was looking upwards too. She had also stumbled out into the murky, empty street and had circled aimlessly. But after a while she had stopped, and begun to listen. And in the muffled silence she'd heard faint voices, like people talking through thick fog, their distance impossible to judge. As she tuned in to the sound, she began to hear footsteps passing hurriedly by and snatches of echoless conversation. Then one footfall caught her attention. It seemed to scuffle unnaturally, to speed up and slow down like someone desperately searching. She followed the footsteps until they stopped by a lamppost, and through the murk she could make out a faint, rasping breath, and then a smell. A musky smell she recognized.

"Reuben," she tried to shout, but her voice was dampened, almost as faint as the ones she could hear.

Reuben sank to the ground, his back against the cold metal of the lamppost, and looked around him, nearly blind with fear. Alma called again, following the faint smell, and lingered at the spot where it seemed to pool. She repeated his name, whispering this time.

"Reuben, I am here."

***

Reuben didn't know why, but he sensed somebody standing there. And then, as he searched, he thought he heard her saying his name, like it had been whispered from inside his own thoughts.

"Alma." As he spoke he felt a light brush on his cheek, as if they were face to face, and he reached out and imagined he could feel her dark, heavy hair flowing through his fingers.

"Alma." The two black orbs of her eyes were suddenly close, almost within him, and then they were there, crying together, body to body on the sunlit pavement, huddled at the base of a lamppost as passers-by looked down at them with distain.

They both lay there, caressing the clanging moment like castaways on a gravelly beach, their bodies rising and falling in unison. Reuben blinked through the orange haze until the street came into focus. Then a familiar figure emerged, the dark green of his army jacket standing out against the grey clothing of the office workers. Like a madman, Theo pawed the air on the far side of the road, as if clearing his way through the hanging vines of an imaginary jungle. He moved slowly out into the flow of traffic, oblivious to the shouts of drivers as they swerved.

110

Every now and then he said something inaudible, his face turned upwards. Reuben crossed the road quickly and pulled Theo back onto the pavement. But Theo continued to move his arms rigidly as Reuben and Alma pushed him back into an alleyway and against a wall.

"Theo. Theo, we're here." Gradually Theo stopped moving, listening intently to the cold air. "Come on, we're here with you." He levelled his gaze, and suddenly recognition passed over his face as he looked from Reuben to Alma sitting in front of him, their faces close and warm in the rose pink evening light.

CHAPTER 19

For a long while nobody spoke, their minds trickling slowly back into the present like sand piling up at the base of an hourglass. Then Theo finally turned towards the others, his eyes kaleidoscopic with fear.

"There's something I should tell you." The words were barely audible over the sounds of the evening street and, unsure if they had heard, Theo spoke again, more forcefully, drawing himself up against the damp panel of a metal dumpster that was rammed against the wall behind him. "I think I know what's going on." He looked at them carefully. Reuben nodded back, his eyes flickering into life as Theo told them how he had seen someone searching his flat all those weeks ago. How he had sat, hunched against the cold tiles of the railway terminal, and used the code to hunt them across the Internet. He told them about the blank web page that had cut his pursuit short, about the mocking face that had leered back at him from the blackness of the empty screen and sent him running mad with fear into the long drunken nights. And, as evening fell across the city, Reuben and Alma began to finally piece together the unsettling events that had led Theo to them.

"And when we first met, on the bridge that night?" Alma leaned forward, drawing with her a cape of shadow from the crumbling wall behind.

"That's where I got my inspiration," Theo said quietly. "I wrote the code as soon as I got home, and the first time I sent it out to trawl the network, they came and searched my apartment."

Reuben stood up abruptly and walked over to the top of the alleyway.

"It's like the world we know can't give us answers anymore," he said, looking out into the night. At the end of the street he could see that the watcher had returned, leaning casually against a wall, the top half of their body hidden in shadows like a villain from a black and white movie. The man shifted from one foot to the other as if he could sense Reuben's eyes on him. Then he turned directly towards the entrance of the alleyway, and Reuben pulled back quickly into the darkness. "We need to get out of here," he said suddenly.

"Look." Alma had also stood up, and was submerged in the shadows at the far end of the alleyway. A pitted, blackened wall blocked it off, but she gestured upwards to where a small window looked out over the brickwork a story up. "We can get in there," she said, pulling one of the bins over. Then she scrambled up on top of it, her feet clanging on the empty metal, and reached over the lintel. She pinched at the rotting wood for a moment, pulling it away from the frame with short, jerky motions. The latch came free and she grasped the sill and pulled herself forwards, hanging as she scrabbled for a foothold against the brickwork. Then she disappeared into the darkness. Reuben and Theo climbed after her uncertainly, the metal bin scraping and banging underneath them.

For a moment the velvet darkness seemed suffocating. Theo held up his mobile phone, but it took several seconds for the outlines of the building to emerge while their eyes adjusted to the faint bluish light. Beyond the entrance hall, a grand staircase plunged into the blackness. Faded, smiling faces looked down menacingly from the walls. Alma took Reuben by the hand and the three of them began to pick their way into the blackness, the old staircase creaking underneath them as they went.

"Listen...." Reuben's voice seemed to ripple in the treacle-thick shadow. "I've been thinking. I mean, whoever they are, why do they react like that every time we use Theo's code?"

They had reached the bottom of the stairway and Theo held the phone up in the air again as they tried to see what was ahead of them. But the darkness just absorbed the pale light and they edged forwards slowly until Alma stumbled.

"Shit, steps." They began to make their way down again. Rows of chair backs emerged from the darkness on either side, lining the walkway as they picked their way slowly towards the front of the abandoned auditorium.

"The code, it terrifies them when we use it, right?" Reuben said as they moved through the darkness. "It means it's damn powerful, I mean, why don't we turn it against them?"

Reuben stopped as a faint tinkle of broken glass interrupted his train of thought.

"Shit, they're in here with us." Fear dripped like black liquid from Alma's voice.

The air seemed to vibrate as they moved forward now. Then, without warning, the auditorium suddenly flashed blood-red as the grand chandeliers began to strobe overhead. There was a shout, and then dark figures were climbing over the chair backs towards them in the flickering crimson light. Reuben had moved ahead and was already on the stage, his face pale as he pulled back the velvet stage curtain silently. In staccato movements he fell forwards, and then disappeared into the floor. Theo and Alma grappled the woodwork behind him and quickly followed him through the small trapdoor and down a narrow staircase, which led directly underneath the varnished stage floor. Theo pulled the wooden hatch closed behind them and raised his phone into the air. Its faint, fading light revealed a corridor, so low that they had to stoop, doors lining the sides. Reuben picked one and kicked it open in a cloud of dust. Then they huddled into an old dressing room and Reuben eased the door carefully shut again. There they waited, their hearts pounding in the darkness as footsteps thundered overhead.

**

Theo had pulled himself under a table that was pushed up against the back wall. As he lay there in the darkness, he became aware of an infinitesimal breeze across his face. He reached out to the wall and felt a cold ridge of air around the edge of one of the wooden panels. It seemed to move when he leaned against it, and so he curled his fingers around the edge and pulled it backwards. It came clear of the wall easily, revealing a hole where the bricks had been knocked through. The gap was just big enough for a person, he thought, and beyond the wall there was darkness, an empty space. He reached out with his leg and kicked Reuben, who crawled over to look. Theo held his phone out into the darkness and waved it backwards and forwards. The chamber below seemed easily large enough for them.

Theo handed the phone to Reuben without speaking and turned himself around as footsteps seemed to pause directly above them. Then he pushed his legs backwards over the edge and eased himself down into the darkness. He couldn't feel anything below, and when he had gone as far as he could, he stopped and looked back at Reuben, his fingers slipping against the damp bricks. Then he let go, and for a brief moment he was in freefall. Then he hit the damp ground, and all he could see was the small square of the phone screen as Reuben waved it into the darkness above him.

"I'm okay," he hissed as loudly as he dared. The phone spiraled downwards towards him, sending small shadows dancing along the walls of what appeared to be an old brick tunnel. Theo picked it up and pointed it towards Reuben and Alma as they prepared to jump. He felt the breeze again, more forcefully this time, and on the wind he could hear a faint clashing sound.

Once they were all on the ground, Theo felt for Reuben's shoulder, and then gripped it as he turned off the light. At the end of the tunnel the blackness merged into pale grey, and they began to pick their way blindly towards it. The dry breeze grew stronger as they advanced, bringing with it the smell of metal and carbon, which overlaid the mushroomy odor of dark, damp soil. There was something else riding the breeze along the ancient brickwork. The sound was hard to define at first, but as their ears adjusted as they advanced, it formed itself into the sound of metal on metal, the sound of motion, until Reuben stopped suddenly and spoke, for the first time in what seemed like hours.

"It's the trains," he said, smiling to himself. "We're in the underground system."

They quickened their pace over the uneven ground, every now and then stumbling blindly on a loose brick that had fallen from the tunnel walls. At the end, another tunnel cut directly across their path, and when they reached the junction the air began to shake as another train screamed past, throwing the smell of hot metal over them, their faces flickering grimly in the passing light from the carriage windows.

"Listen," Reuben shouted over the sound of the disappearing train. "I know what to do. Just wait for me here, I'll come back in a while." Then, without warning, he turned into the eddying air and disappeared into the darkness.

Theo and Alma didn't speak as they waited, sitting against the wall on opposite sides of the tunnel, drifting in and out of consciousness. Bit by bit the lingering pauses between each train seemed to stretch as the night deepened overhead. After a while it got colder, and Theo could hear Alma shivering in the darkness. He wriggled out of his army jacket and threw it across the damp floor to her. A little later Reuben returned, the flash of his grin preceding him as he scuffled along the edge of the tunnel. He handed them each a damp gas-station sandwich, and then passed around a warm can of beer. As they ate, he sat in silence, smiling to himself.

"What's so funny?" Alma asked finally.

Reuben looked up, startled for a moment, as if he had forgotten that they were there.

"Oh, well, it's just…." Reuben trailed off for a second. "It's just that…well, you'll see. I've arranged a few things. You're going to like it." His words were cut short as another train thundered past in the darkness, its windows throwing strobed yellow light into the tunnel as the three of them crouched against the sooty black wall like vagabonds. When the light faded again, Reuben stood and began to make his way after the train. Theo and Alma scrambled after him out into the main tunnel, their legs aching from the long wait. There was no walkway, and they made their way carefully along the narrow space at the side of the track, but after a moment Theo stopped and shouted forward.

"But wait, what if a train comes?" he yelled into the darkness ahead of him.

"Yeah, just hurry up." Reuben's voice was faint; he was already further away than Theo expected. "It's only a little way."

Theo pushed on, focusing his thoughts on the reassuring crunch of their footsteps against the gravel as they made their way through the darkness, each step producing a sharp sound of stone against stone, which rang for an instant as it echoed off the brick walls. That's why Theo took some time to untangle a second ringing that pulsed along the metal rails from the cloud of noise. But as soon as he picked out the sound of the approaching train he shouted up to Reuben and began to run. By now the pulsing on the track had become so loud that he didn't hear Reuben's reply as his feet pounded desperately against the loose stones.

Moments later the tunnel seemed to be on fire with dancing light. Reuben and Alma were nowhere to be seen, and Theo shouted out desperately as the wind from the approaching train pushed him forward, the smell of hot metal and burning dust filling the screaming air. The driver sounded the horn at the blackened figure running rabbit-like in front of him in the glare. Then, just as the front of the train was upon him, a hand reached out and pulled Theo aside, wrenching him into a black space that had opened up along the edge of the tunnel. Theo looked around, shivering with fear, but Reuben was still grinning crazily at him, his eyes aflame in the flickering light.

"I told you to run," he said, laughing like a madman. Alma's face was also drawn white with fear. After a moment it was quiet again, and Reuben stepped back into the tunnel. "The station's just up there." He pointed into the darkness and began to run. This time Theo and Alma followed close behind, the sound of their footfalls crashing almost in unison. After a few moments, they turned a corner and fell into the glare of a station, scrambling quickly up onto the platform, black-faced and breathless.

A few of the waiting passengers stole glances at the three of them as they caught their breath at the end of the platform, their clothes sooty and torn from the inside of the tunnel. After a while another breeze began to sweep along the tiles, and Reuben placed his hand on Theo's shoulder as the last train of the night

121

came thundering around the bend. They stepped into the carriage and stood silently at one end as the train continued its thunderous journey, twisting into the blackness of the tunnel.

CHAPTER 20

It was hard to tell if Razer was more bored or disgusted as he stood among the scattered rubbish in front of the underground station, his hands clasped in front of him around the handle of a black bag. When he saw Reuben and the others emerge, he stepped forward quickly and held out the bag, anxious to get rid of it.

"Where have you been?" Razer said.

No one replied as they stood there huddled in the cold, orange night. In their exhaustion everything suddenly seemed unreal, like the two-dimensional façade of a movie set, as if Razer was just reading out lines from a script. Behind them the deserted station seemed to brace itself, the sheer walls of warehouses looming away into the darkness behind it.

"So what the fuck are we doing here?" This time Razer spat the words out into the night air, the sharp edge of the obscenity flipping them back into the present with a jolt.

"You'll see," Reuben said suddenly. He took the bag and turned towards one of the darkened side streets that led away from the station. As they stepped out from under the canopy of orange light, they caught snatches of a twisting, urgent bassline riding on the night wind. Reuben cut quickly through the darkness, winding his way past the containers and padlocked fences.

"What the hell is he up to?" Razer looked over to Theo and Alma, who both shrugged back at him in the darkness.

After a while they came to a group of vans parked up close against the side of one of the warehouses. The undulating bassline filled the air now, gyrating and thundering into the night. Reuben disappeared into the shadows between the vans while the others waited for him, huddled uncertainly in the grey light. Behind the vehicles, three figures were only visible by the red tips of their cigarettes in the darkness. Reuben came back after a few seconds and beckoned for the others to follow him. Then he muttered something to one of the men, who pulled back the corrugated metal where the fence had been cut.

Inside a fire burned in the middle of the overgrown courtyard, and small groups of people stood around talking in the flickering light. The music flowed over them from an abandoned factory that stood in the darkness, lights flashing out into the night from the empty window frames. Reuben led them into the entryway, and as they crossed the threshold, a girl with braided hair looked up at him and winked. The stairway was full of people selling drugs in the darkness, and they pushed their way through the crowd up onto the first floor, where music pounded into the room. It was totally dark except for the strobe light, which made the dancers look as if their movements were jolted and unnatural.

As they reached the middle of the crammed dance floor, the music reached a peak and paused. Reuben and the others stopped too, for an instant in tune with the crowd, and then as the music cascaded forward again they pushed across to the edge of the room to where a shaven-headed man waited for them. He punched his fist against Reuben's and shouted something, and then pushed open a door behind him and Reuben gestured for the others to step through. They made their way up a narrow flight of stairs and along a corridor to an empty room at the end. Once they were inside, Reuben jammed the door shut with a piece of wood, clouds of dust filling the air as he kicked it fast.

"We'll be safe here," he shouted over the music thundering underneath them, giving the plank a final kick. The others looked back at him, bemused.

"Mate, what the hell are we doing here?" Razer shouted back at him.

Reuben smiled and reached into the bag, and began to pull out laptop computers and pass them around.

"Look, whoever is following us doesn't want us to use the code. That means it's powerful; it means we can do some real damage with it." He gestured towards Theo, who had stood back from the others and was leaning against the wall, his face white and drawn in the dim light. "He has already tried to use it to hunt them down, but he could not succeed alone. But if we use it all at the same time, here where they can't get at us, well...maybe we'll be able to find out what the fuck is going on."

Theo shrugged, lowered himself against the bare brick wall, and began to type. As he did so he shouted out the code to the others, their faces ghostly in the blue light from the computer screens. He sent them each the program that would carry the code across the network, then he led them back through the same digital tunnels he had traversed weeks ago. Through Transcom, the corrupt transport company that had given away his journey across the city, and back through the cascade of temporary email address, until they came up against the same blank web page. Theo shivered as he looked back into the darkness of the empty page and remembered the face that had leered back at him in the station. But this time the software pushed forward, and the darkness of the page began to clear, and as it did so, an image of a small room appeared. Reuben gasped; it was the room they were sitting in now. And as they stared right back at themselves, speechless with disbelief, the music below them suddenly faded into silence.

CHAPTER 21

Reuben ran his hand along the cold, rough surface of the metal underneath him as he gazed out across the fog. He could just about make out the old building, the outline of its broken walls silhouetted against the pale light. The banks of fog parted momentarily to reveal the derelict city beyond, before enclosing it again in an undulating landscape of grey and white. Around the globe of light that surrounded him, Reuben could sense the darkness shifting and chattering, yet he felt a deep peacefulness radiating through him as he turned his body sideways across the rusted surface of the old girder and lowered himself until just his fingers gripped the edge. Then he let go, and began to fall slowly through the thick air, the darkness parting underneath him as he descended. After a moment, his feet grazed the gravelly earth with a muted crunch. The air was cooler at ground level, and he could feel a slow breeze against his forehead as he picked his way slowly across the empty courtyard to the furrow where the fencing had stood. The ground was rough and pitted, as if nothing had happened there for an eon, but as he stepped across the threshold he heard his name echoing from far away.

"Reu-b-en."

It was as if someone was shouting to him from the other end of a long tube. He stopped and strained to hear through the deadening fog.

"Reuu-ben."

This time it was louder, then the light shifted behind him and he turned to see Alma standing luminescent, her body encased in a halo of milky light. Then it cracked into gold as she smiled and beckoned to him.

"Check thi-s ou-ut."

Reuben stumbled backwards as Alma rose spectrally into the air like a comic book Madonna.

"Com-onnn," she shouted faintly. He looked down at his feet, and then sprung upwards, gasping as the ground receded underneath him. Reuben stretched forward, and then he could feel the thick, damp air suddenly rushing across his face as he streamed upwards, the old city falling away below him. Alma looked at him gleefully and cackled as they soared upwards until the city was spread far below them, the blackness broken every now and then with small lights bursting like tiny fireworks.

Reuben suddenly felt as if ghostly particles were rushing past him and out into the inky sky. He looked across at Alma, who grinned and rolled over slowly and then stretched forwards, arching her back as she swooped back down towards the flickering city, her trajectory leaving a small trail through the mist.

Reuben turned after her and the two of them careered over the buildings, dipping into the canyon-like streets as they furrowed their way across the deserted city. As they went, the light from their bodies cut through the darkness and sent jagged shadows arching across the broken buildings, until finally, they doubled back towards the warehouse, cutting directly across the crumbling rooftops. When the building came into sight, they slowed and Reuben stretched out his hand to run it along an adjoining wall as they passed. But then he pulled it back quickly as if he had hurt himself. Where he'd touched it, the brickwork had disintegrated into an arc of broken masonry that hung almost motionless in the grey air. Alma came to rest next to him and they stood, speechless for a moment as they looked at the surreal spectacle. But then a shifting light behind them caught Reuben's attention. It suddenly felt as if someone else was looking at it too, and Reuben turned to see a small blur quickly draw away, fragmenting as it moved between the columns of broken wall.

He followed, anxious to catch it before it disappeared into the fog. The ground beyond the roadway was littered with artefacts from the world they had left behind, shards of plastic, bent metal, fading pages of magazines crumpled into the dirt. Reuben moved forward slowly through the rubble, following the milky cloud at a distance. Then the light seemed to stop, and for a while Reuben lingered also, waiting behind a blackened pillar of tumbledown bricks. Finally he stepped out into the clearing, and across the rough ground he could see it was Theo, pacing in madman circles under the gaping archway of a fallen wall.

He walked towards his friend, but as he reached the other side, Reuben suddenly stopped, pulled up by the sound of distant voices on the damp wind. It was as if the tear-filled breeze itself was heavy with a cargo of lonely souls that it hauled across the derelict city. Reuben stood there in the semi-darkness while the sound of despair whistled in his ears like silence, and then he began to cry. Theo had stopped pacing and looked directly at Reuben, tears streaming down his face too, and in that moment of understanding the two men listened together to the bitter harmonies that wove into the mist.

"Caa-m on." Alma suddenly broke the spell, and they gathered themselves for a moment and then moved slowly into the shroud of the building. Alma led them back across the deserted hall and up the small staircase to the room. The door hung limply from its hinges, the wood long rotten and crumbled. But as they stood there, they could still see imprints in the dust at the places where they had been, their invisible bodies casting faint shadows across the floor. Reuben stepped across to the back wall where he had sat, and as he bent over the clearing in the dirt, a taste of dust filled his mouth as the air rushed past him and he fell forwards.

CHAPTER 22

There was a roaring sound, the deafening crash of masonry, and Reuben knew he was going to vomit. He reached blindly to the right until he could feel the damp brickwork under his fingers and tried to turn his head, but his stomach convulsed before he could complete the movement and he raised himself just enough to let the thick, bitter liquid roll over the dust underneath him and seep into the gaps in the floorboards. Then he pushed himself across to the wall, the rough wood against his face, and rotated until he was sitting upright then opened his eyes.

An offset grid...no, two. Each one was shifting, rotating. He blinked and tried again. This time they synchronized, cement lines on the wall opposite. Underneath lay Alma, rocking slowly back and forth, her face in her hands. Reuben tried to move his eyes, but at first they resisted. He strained for a moment against the pain. Behind Alma the door was back on its hinges and jammed shut. Next to it Razer leaned face in against the wall and threw up. Then there was a deafening caterwaul from downstairs as a needle cut laterally across the grooves of a vinyl record. There were shouts, but Reuben couldn't hear what they were saying over the buzz of feedback from the sound system. He tried to stand, but his legs could not hold him and he fell sideways onto the floor, landing directly in front of Theo, who sat with his back to the wall, staring straight ahead.

Someone hammered on the door and shouted. There was panic in the voice, and Reuben tried to stand again, pushing back against the brick, more slowly this time, steadying himself carefully. The voices outside had become louder, more urgent, and behind the shouts Reuben could make out approaching sirens. He pulled himself across to the window and smeared away the dust with his sleeve. Outside the fire was still burning, but everyone was jostling against the fence, trying to push through the small opening and out into the street. There was panic on their faces, and Reuben pushed his head up against the window pane, but he could not see far enough around the building. Then he turned quickly into the darkened room and fell forwards again as his legs collapsed. He got back up shakily and lunged this time at the mottled iron door latch across the room.

The hallway was dark and empty now, and Reuben pushed his arms crossways against its walls to steady himself as he inched forwards to the stairway. Razer and Alma were behind him, and in the flashes of blue light that arched along the walls Reuben could see their faces, wrought in fear like church gargoyles. But Theo was missing.

"Where the hell is he?" Reuben thought, or spoke, he wasn't sure. The corridor was barely two shoulders wide, and he pushed clumsily back past the other two to the doorway and into the small room where they had all been sitting. Theo was still there, curled up against the crumbling wall. To Reuben, his face suddenly seemed unfamiliar, shifting, as if a kaleidoscope of souls was swirling inside a vacant body. "Come on," Reuben tried to shout, but his words were gasping and hoarse, and he stepped across the dust and pulled at Theo's arm. Theo suddenly roused, coughing, and looked up at him in bewilderment. "We've got to go." Reuben's voice was stronger now, and Theo rose zombie-like, his face almost translucent in the dim light.

They picked their way carefully back down the

staircase and into the now empty hall. Radiating squares of electric blue light streaked along the ceiling as they advanced into the deserted dance floor.

***

They weren't aware of it, but the shifting light picked up something else that followed them out of the doorway, something only visible in the thin eddies of air that caused the crumpled cigarette packets and plastic bottles to shift imperceptibly against the old floorboards.

***

By the time they reached the courtyard, the police had already breached the compound. A blonde girl tried to push through, but two uniforms pulled her roughly to the floor, a dark-blue knee pushed into her neck as she lay immobile in the dirt. Reuben looked at her face and saw that she had started to cry, her tears glistening grey in the silver light of early dawn. Reuben had been gripping onto Theo's upper arm while they moved across the broken paving stones, but as they rounded the edge of the building he dropped it. Where Reuben had touched the wall, the adjoining warehouse had collapsed into the street, throwing rubble out along the roadway and crushing the fence that divided the two buildings. A wave of policemen was moving towards them across the fallen masonry, and Reuben turned to look at Alma, who stared back at him, her eyes unmoving.

Theo was fully awake now, and he put his arm back across Reuben's shoulder.

"Come on, let's get the hell out of here."

They turned back and began to follow another group around to the other side of the building, and then over a rusted mesh fence into the darkness of the street. At the end of the fence, a concrete wall marked the start of the next plot, and in between the two, a gangly bush had forced its way out onto the pavement, its branches spilling over the fence out onto the sidewalk. It was there that Reuben stopped, sinking down to the floor and letting the tattered branches fall around his head.

"Fuck," he said finally into his hands. "How the hell did I do that?"

"It's like we were totally powerful there, like it didn't take any effort," Alma said, almost to herself.

Razer had been standing slightly back from the rest of them, but now he stepped forward until he was directly in front of Reuben.

"Yeah, okay, but what the hell was that?"

For a moment none of them spoke, their minds still lingering along the boundary between worlds, until Theo finally broke the silence.

"I think I know what happened to us." He spoke so softly that for a moment no one realized he had said anything at all. Alma turned to him slowly.

"What, what do you mean?"

"I think I've seen that place before." His words were unsure, hesitant. "You were there." He looked down at Alma, who had sat on the pavement next to Reuben. "The night when you saved my life on the bridge, I must have knocked myself out, and I dreamed of the exact same place."

Alma looked at the floor silently, and in the grey light that drew them all in monochrome silhouettes she tried to hide her face. Then finally she spoke again, her voice softened almost to a whisper.

"Theo, I didn't save you."

"Yes, I remem—"

"No, I tried to." Alma cut him off. "But I couldn't hold you. You fell. By the time I made it down to the water, someone had pulled you out, but you weren't…." She stopped, afraid to go on. "They tried to revive you, but I thought you weren't going to make it, Theo, I really did. Then the look in your eyes when you finally woke up and started coughing…." For a moment they all stood in silence as the dawn advanced along the almost deserted street. Theo turned away, his black eyes blending into the shadows.

"You mean…." He stumbled, unable to complete the sentence. Alma nodded silently, and around them the fading darkness seemed to seethe and shift.

CHAPTER 23

Theo fell behind the others as they made their way back towards the city lights, his thoughts lingering in the uncomfortably familiar world they had just left. He was at least a block away by the time they reached the concrete columns of the overpass that led back into the city. They waited for him on the entry ramp, watching silently as he advanced through the undulating light, his hands deep in the pockets of his tattered coat. A taxi emerged from the darkened streets, its headlamps suddenly illuminating their waiting faces. Razer hailed it impatiently, and he was already talking to the driver when Theo reached them, his breath heavy in the cold night air, and pulled Reuben to one side.

"Listen, I think I'm gonna walk for a while," he

whispered.

"No, man, that's not a good idea." Reuben put his hand on Theo's shoulder as he spoke, but Theo pulled away and stepped backwards into the shadows.

"I'll see you soon."

The others had already gotten into the cab, and when Reuben turned back, Theo was a hundred yards away, walking head down into the gallery of columns underneath the raised roadway. As Reuben watched, Theo turned and cast a final look at him. By now his face was just a smudge in the dirty grey dawn, but as Reuben pulled the car door closed he had the unsettling impression that Theo had been trying to tell him something.

The taxi funneled back into the dome of early morning lights, the streets blurring into pale grey as they sat in silence, absorbed in the events that had brought them to this point. It was Alma who finally broke the spell, turning pale faced towards the others.

"Where was that place?" Her voice was hushed. "I mean, it was like we were here, but in another time or something."

"In a bloody nightmare, more like." Razer had been leaning against the window, staring blackly out into the passing streets, but as he turned to look across Reuben to Alma, his face suddenly seemed unreal in the phasing orange light. Alma was silent

141

for a while, deep in thought as the taxi moved across the city. Then finally she turned back to the other two.

"I always suspected it, you know." They both looked back across at her, unsure what to think. "I mean, it's obvious in a way. The world we live in has to be an illusion; it has to be unreal because of infinity."

Razer shrugged and turned back to look out of the window and watch the grey streets pass by, but Reuben steadied himself against the seat back as the taxi turned off the causeway and cut into the mesh of city streets.

"What do you mean?"

"Well, if you think about it, the universe must have an end, an edge, right? And yet there can never be an end because there must always be something afterwards." Alma was leaning forward now, her face momentarily illuminated in the passing streetlights. "It's a paradox. It makes the three-dimensional space we think we live in logically impossible. And if that's true, then there must be something more, another world alongside our own."

Razer suddenly broke the conversation to lean forwards and tap the plastic screen with irritation as the taxi turned into one of the long illuminated underpasses that led into the financial district.

"Not that way, mate," he shouted through the

small holes, but the driver did not react, his black-suited form immobile as he burrowed the car deeper into the city. Razer leaned across Reuben and tapped the plastic again, insisting this time, and without warning the driver slammed the brakes hard. The car began to slide against the tarmac with a squeal, and when it had come to rest, the driver turned to look at them across the Perspex.

It was then that they saw his face, the skin unnaturally white and drawn, two sunken black hollows where his eyes should have been. On each side of the bench seat, Razer and Alma began to tear at the door handles desperately, but they were locked. A faint smile formed across the driver's narrow lips as he watched them struggle for a moment, and then he turned back to the road and pushed the car forward again as the skyscrapers rose around them like giant tombstones. They continued to shout and hammer against the glass as the car glided silently into the city, but fell quiet when it turned into the cavernous bowel of one of the vast buildings, spiraling downwards to a deserted garage. None of them spoke as the vacant parking lots passed by, each more portentous than the last, until the taxi came to rest against a flat concrete wall at the end and the driver turned again, his face black with shadows, and released the latch.

They huddled together in the near darkness a

few feet away from the car, while all around them the shadows seemed to move and undulate. The driver got out behind them and slammed his door shut, the sharp noise reverberating back down the long hallway. Then, as they stood there, the shadows began to gather and pool in front of them, as if an invisible mass was rising out of the concrete floor.

"Run." Reuben threw the word behind him as he started headlong back through the parking lot. A rushing noise filled the air, and behind them a wave of blackness crashed through the empty lots. Then Reuben felt a hand on his shoulder, and fell forward onto the concrete floor. He felt the taste of a musty cloth as a bag was pulled over his head, and he was pressed facedown while his hands were bound together behind him with plastic strips. The cloth was tight against his face, and he breathed hard as they pulled him to his feet again and began to push him forwards. Reuben could hear heavy breathing around him as they walked, then they stopped for a moment while a door was opened. Reuben tried to shout, "Alma." He heard a muffled reply, followed by the metallic ring of lift doors sliding open. They stepped into the echoing interior, and Reuben felt suddenly giddy as the lift accelerated. He tried to feel around him with the side of his arm, but a hand pushed him forward against the lift wall. "Get the fuck off me." Reuben threw his head backwards blindly, and in reply came an explosion of pain across the top of his skull.

When he awoke again he could taste blood. He was slumped forward in a chair, his arms stretched painfully behind him around the wooden back. He tried to look up, and through the rough mesh of cotton he thought he could see a figure standing in front of him. Reuben swayed his head left and right to catch the shadows so he could see better. There was a muffled shout, and then his view darkened as if others were gathering round.

"We've been watching you and your friends for a while." The metallic voice seemed to come from one side, and Reuben tried to turn his head, but he couldn't see. "Hiss, click. Why have you been so insistent?" Each utterance started and ended with a mechanical noise, almost like an old-time cassette player.

"Hiss tch-click. Ask about the code," another, different voice interrupted.

"The code you have been using, where did you learn it?"

Reuben leaned forward. "Who the hell are you?" He was shouting, but it sounded faint and breathless. "I won't tell you anything."

"We must know about the code, please. Where

did you learn it?" The impassive, mechanical tone revealed no emotion, but Reuben was trying to stand, his breath taut with fury.

"Why should I talk to you?" Someone pushed him back into the chair.

"We need to know where you learned the code, we must know it."

"I'll tell you once you let me go." Reuben tried to sound calmer this time. He leaned forward and felt a hand against his chest again. "Otherwise I'll say nothing."

"Htishh, tclick. Hahahahahaha." It sounded like a computer reading out the words more than a laugh. "We will let you go soon, I promise, hahahaha. But I need to know. How did you learn the code? Where did you see it?"

Reuben did not speak now. He could hear mumbling, and the voice addressed someone else a few feet away.

"Mr. Theo, where did you learn the code you have been using?"

"I'm not bloody Theo." Razer spat the words out stupidly, and Reuben heard the scraping noise of a chair being pulled back, and then the sound of scuffling. The chair fell to the floor and there was murmuring again. Then the voice came back to Reuben.

"Hissss tclick. Where is your friend Mr. Theo?"

Reuben didn't answer.

"Click." Reuben waited, unnerved by the pause. "Tell us, where is Mr. Theo? We must know," the voice said after a few moments in the same emotionless monotone.

Reuben decided not to talk anymore, and he let each breath rise and fall slowly as the silence filled the air around them.

"We must know, please. It means everything to us. Answer, or you will regret it, I promise."

Reuben paused between each breath, and felt strangely peaceful as he listened to the expectant, empty moment. Then there was a hand on his back, and he was pulled upright and pushed forward across the room. He could feel cool air against his skin now as the hand pulled him upwards again, and Reuben stumbled against the tall step. He regained his footing and went to move forward, but the hand held him, pushing him sideways.

"Not yet. Hahahaha. Please, this is your last chance."

Reuben shook his head and smiled to himself defiantly.

"As you wish. You are free to go now. Hahaha."

Then there was a definitive clicking sound, and Reuben stood motionless for a moment, listening.

147

The air was cooler now, and he stepped forward gingerly, feeling for the ground as his weight shifted. As he did so an updraft of air momentarily raised the bottom edge of the hood and his heart lurched. In that flash, he saw the streets like matchsticks far below, and he tried to throw himself backwards against the wall, but it was already too late. His back foot slipped forward and he began to fall, spiraling into the void, his body rigid with terror.

CHAPTER 24

The long shadows seemed to absorb Theo as he sidestepped the headlamp glare of the taxi and gathered his frayed herringbone coat against the driving wind. He let the slow arc of the roadway guide him along the city's edge while Alma's words rang shrill in his mind like a distant alarm. He could remember her intonation precisely as they had stood, nauseous with fear on the edge of the night. He tried to reason their implications, but his unmarshalled thoughts swirled around him like the rubbish that clattered against the columns underneath the concrete roadway. For a while he let time move forward, pacing it out as the darkened warehouses gave way to blank terraces, crooked and grey with soot, until the stumbling metronome of his footsteps began to settle his mind on the moment it had buried during the terrifying, cascading past few months. He carefully replayed it, remembering how he had stood on the edge of the bridge and watched two points form on the surface of the churning black river. Then he tried to bury deeper, to peel away the layers of memory and reveal what had happened next. But there was nothing, a void. He was unable to retrieve it from the storybook of his mind.

As he walked, Theo didn't notice the overpass splitting overhead and arching down on either side of him to meld into the tarmac walkway. He didn't see the blustery morning steal away, and he was suddenly surprised to feel weak sunlight falling against his skin. Theo stopped and looked up into the clear blue air, the moment crystallizing around him as he stood, a disheveled figure against the bright winter day, golden hexagons of sunlight strafing his vision. In that moment, as Theo's paper-pale skin began to glow, he suddenly felt his own existence envelop him like a warm towel.

"Fuck." The word dissipated immediately in the dry air, and he smiled at himself as he stopped to rest against a wall, his thoughts gathering unbidden around the one thing that had given him meaning all along. As he looked out across the bright suburban street, at the winter flowers that suddenly seemed to materialize along the brickwork opposite, he realized that Roxana was the only thing he had ever loved, and that in his delusion he had let her slip from his grasp.

The moment of clarity pushed Theo to his feet again and, suddenly resolved, he turned and cut directly across the traffic, back towards the towering city. He sliced through the cluttered and haphazard streets, along the shouting markets, past the somber gaze of dark-windowed pubs, the young, determined mothers, through the reddening day, and finally back into the canyon of the city where steel and glass cut upwards into the sky.

Along the way he obtained a computer, this time leaping almost absent-mindedly through the shop alarm and jumping across the roaring traffic, his train of thought barely fluctuating as the security guard shouted hopelessly after him. He tucked the machine under his arm as he weaved through the crowd on the pavement opposite, then he turned the final block and lowered himself against the glass window of one of the city coffee bars and jacked into the wireless network as he took up watch on the office building across the street.

It wasn't long before a familiar yellow smudge

appeared through the semi-opaque glass as Roxana descended the escalator of the office block and approached the security gates in the lobby. As soon as he saw her, Theo pointed the software at the blank page again, and gradually the darkness of the empty page cleared to reveal an image of the road in front of him as the screeching world faded away and he was left sitting in the murky silence of the deserted street. Shuddering with the transition, Theo pushed himself away from his position on the pavement and rolled slowly out across the street to the towering entrance of the derelict building, its steel frame bent and warped from the centuries, its gleaming panels of glass long gone. He came to rest against the cracked marble floor and walked forwards slowly as if he was wading through deep water. As he walked, he listened to the whispering souls that remained suspended there, like snatches of conversation from a distant radio, until he caught her soft murmur in the still air. He paused for a moment, letting her intoxicating aura wash over him, and then kicked off and out into the street. Theo had spotted a flower stall a block away, and he twisted himself through the heavy air to where the remnants of the wooden cart still stood, tipped backwards against the collapsed pavement. Theo lifted the whole thing and moved it slowly across to the entrance of her building. Then he turned upwards, spiraling along the crooked frame of the skyscraper, pulling the cart behind him. When he reached the top edge, where the thick fog formed a bow wave against the giant building, he reversed, and let himself fall downwards again, the bent girders whistling past.

At the last moment, he twisted his feet backwards and landed on the pavement to haul the broken cart soundlessly back to its position tipped against the curb. Then he sank back into the small dark patch at the foot of the cafe window as the street jarred back into life. He swallowed back the nausea of the transition for a moment, and then stood and crossed the clanging roadway to meet her.

Roxana had just stepped through the barriers when she saw him, sickly and disheveled, loitering outside the entranceway. For a moment she looked away, embarrassed, saddened, but Theo stepped forward anyway, putting his hand lightly on her elbow as she tried to bustle past him.

"What's up, Theo?" Her eyes darkened at the intrusion. "I don't want to see you anymore, remember?"

Theo hesitated for a moment, suddenly thrown back by her directness, and he mumbled confusedly. Then he tried again, clearing his throat and tightening his grip on her arm.

"Wait, please. I need to tell you that I'm really sorry." Roxana stopped, taken aback by the unexpected apology. Theo pulled her toward him, his voice softening. "I'm really sorry that I didn't realize how much I loved you, how much we loved each other." Roxana was almost pressed against him as the first disc of pink landed on the pavement. "Forgive me," he whispered, and bent forwards to kiss her as the cloud of falling flower petals began to turn the street around them pink and crimson.

CHAPTER 25

He could still picture her naked body in the undulating rhythm of the falling shower water as he stretched across the hotel bed and looked out at the glistening city spread below. As he waited, Theo luxuriated in the animal smell that still lingered in the room, remembering in it the feel of her skin against him just a few moments earlier. Then he heard her turn off the water and saw the light shift through the open door of the bathroom as she stepped, dripping, from the cubicle and padded across the tiles to the sink.

Theo pulled the laptop from the bedside table and gathered the pillows into a ball, which he jammed behind him against the chocolate leather headboard. Then he brought up the empty page again and released the software, and watched the color drain from the hotel room. A damp, grey wind whistled through the bent window frame of the suddenly decaying building as Theo stood uncertainly where the bed had been, and stepped across the uneven floor to pull at the bathroom door. It fell noiselessly to the floor, and standing there on the broken tiles, Theo could just about hear her thoughts in the harmonies of air that swirled around the empty cavity. He gripped the cracked basin and began to write in thick letters across the ancient grime that caked the surface of the mirror.

"COME BACK TO BED X, T." The uneven capital letters seemed to trail away as he reached the end, and he had to cram the last one in against the tarnished, broken faucets. Then Theo stepped quickly into the bedroom and sank back into the faint shadow of himself against the wall. The room lurched sickeningly back into view just in time for him to see the bathroom door fly open and look at her as she stood there, her golden breasts rising and falling in incredulity.

"What?" She paused, her hand white-knuckled against the door lintel. "How the hell did you do that?" Theo grinned so hard it almost hurt as he stood up and gestured towards the computer lying open on the bed.

"Look, I'll show you." He draped a hotel bathrobe over her narrow shoulders and led her back across the thick pile carpet to the bed. She sat in front of him between his legs, and kissed him as he tried to position the laptop on the crumpled duvet.

"I'm still competing with that thing, aren't I?" she said half-joking as he reached around her to start typing.

"Wait, just watch this."

She turned towards the machine as the characters began to fill the screen. For a moment they both sat there, the light from the laptop turning their faces faint green as the software bored into the invisible fabric that separated their world from the world that lay beyond the soft lights of the luxury hotel suite. Then they were standing together in the empty shell of the tower block as the wind roared against the gaping window. Theo held Roxana's hand and smiled at her, their faces distorted as time stretched and undulated around them.

"Cheeck thiiis oouut." His voice was barely audible as he led her through the swirling air to the edge of the window and tried to pull her over the lintel and out into the void. But she held back, panicking. "Truust me." Theo let go of her and then stepped out through the window frame and let himself float outside the building, grinning at her as he held out his hand. She reached out slowly, and as soon as their skin made contact across the chasm, he pulled her out of the building and held her against him as they turned slowly in the cool, damp air. Then, without warning, their minds began to intermingle like two liquids coiling down the same plughole. Neither spoke as they collapsed unexpectedly into each other, their thoughts forming a whispering duet. At the same time, they started to rise along the shattered edge of the building, moving faster and faster until they passed over the rooftops and out into the black air, until the city glittered underneath them, until it diminished into a cluster of diamonds on the black velvet fabric of the earth that curved away into darkness.

As they held each other speechless in the penthouse of the world, Theo suddenly heard a familiar sound. He pulled away, and they stopped rising and began to fall slowly back through the thick air. As the city expanded below them like a vast opening eye, Theo suddenly spotted Reuben's cry of terror in small explosions of light above the rising skyscrapers.

"Fuuuck, that's Reu-ben," he shouted over the sound of the air rushing past. "I neeed to goaw." His voice faded as he turned towards the cry, narrowing his eyes against the thick air that howled past his face.

CHAPTER 26

It was like a gothic still-life, Reuben gradually falling from an open window, his foot still reaching backwards for the patterned concrete ledge. Theo circled him, deafened by the cry of terror that had caused the curtain between worlds to billow and part, sending gusts of fear exploding into the shadows. Theo traced Reuben's pathway backwards through time, up onto the windy ledge, pressed among the gargoyles, and back towards the room where they had been interrogated. But just as he reached the sill, Theo suddenly stopped dead. In front of him two gangly shadows lingered on the edge of the light.

"Iiiiit's hiiim." Blackness pooled in the gaping eye sockets as one of them spoke, a tattered shirt sleeve streaming from its arm pointing out of the

159

window at Theo. "Hesss caam for themm."

As Theo pressed forwards again across the threshold, the two dark beings fluttered like cornered ravens and began to move backwards across the cracked floor. Then they were suddenly gone, slipping out through the door at the end and into the carcass of the building. Theo paused to catch his breath, but as he stood next to the window he became aware of another noise, a familiar voice, a sorrowful song riding on the thick air. He inched forward through the dark green light until he reached the point where Alma's voice rested, and stopped to let the melody of her soul lap over him like warm, scented water. As he stood there, Theo caught a glimpse of himself in a broken mirror that had fallen against the wall, his body glowing with thin milky light. He watched himself coalesce for a moment against the shadows, then he turned and ran out of the window and into the cool, streaming air. Once he had reached ground level, he crossed the crumbling tarmac of the roadway and made his way along the side of a raised railway line as he searched for a way to save Reuben. After a few moments, the wall gave way to an archway, and as Theo passed underneath it, he thought he could hear whispering in the echo chamber of crumbling grey bricks. When he reached the far side, he leapt up onto the bank and looked around at the sheer walls of the buildings that rose like sea cliffs out of the mist.

He had a sudden flashback as he paused there. He was much younger, travelling the same railroad, coming home in the early morning, his head still humming from the chemicals that had driven him through the night. He remembered how the dawn had suddenly gathered on the steel and glass of the building opposite and doused him in unexpected yellow light. As the two moments overlapped in his mind, Theo looked up at that same building, its glass long gone, its steel frame buckled with time. Even in the real world, the building had been abandoned, earmarked for demolition, he thought, as a pendulum of dread pulled against his belly and he remembered suddenly how the warehouse had collapsed after Reuben had brushed his hand against it. And like the sudden rumble of an approaching train, an idea formed in his mind.

Theo glanced quickly up to the top of the building, and then back across the far side of the track, measuring the distance with his eye. Then he pushed himself upwards until he reached the top edge of the tower block. Across the chasm he could just about see the open window, and below it the faint shadow of Reuben's slowly falling body. Then Theo jumped out into the slow updraft behind the building. When he was several yards out, he turned

161

and threw himself forwards, shoulder first, until he hit the top of the tower and was thrown backwards as the building shuddered beneath him. Theo tried again and again as the building gradually bent forwards over the railway track below. Finally, with a deafening wrench, the ancient metal tore free and the building fell like a slow-motion domino, sending eddies of thick fog curling around the sides as it slowly leaned in across the chasm. Then it connected to the side of the tower on the far side with the inevitability of a colliding ship, shattered concrete and glass streaming like water onto the street below.

Chapter 27

Alma tried to stand, but underneath her the floor swayed with the force of the impact and she fell backwards onto the chair. The sounds around her were jumbled and confused through the thick cloth of the hood. She tried again, more slowly, as the building shuddered violently around her. Once she had steadied herself, she bent forwards and shook the hood to the floor, and then she was blinking in the sudden, dusty light. She could hear shouting and the tearing of masonry and glass, and she ran through the dust to the open window. The collapsed building had embedded into the art deco frontispiece below her, cars splayed out across the roadway underneath it like discarded toys. Dust streamed from the impact site like jets of steam. In the middle of the street, an aging punk stood looking upwards, a small puddle forming underneath him as he poured his can of beer absent-mindedly onto the ground. Then Alma saw a flash of white along the bent surface, a body rolling along the warped metal, its arms tied behind its back, its face obscured by a cotton hood. She gripped the window frame as she watched Reuben roll along the metal edge and then drop the last few meters onto the tarmac, his back bent awkwardly behind him.

Then she turned back into the room. That was when she saw the machine, squat in the center of the floor, carved chimeric creatures half-submerged in the ancient, blackened wood, frozen long ago in the act of escape. Along the front, a dial ran lengthways above a single speaker grille like an old-style radio. On the other side, a long handle seemed to lever against a pair of bellows. Alma didn't wonder about it for long. Instead she began to kick against the glass screen of the dial until it cracked. Then she dislodged a shard with the side of her boot and, grunting with the effort, bent backwards and scraped the broken glass along the plastic cord that pinned her hands together. And then she was free. In front of her Razor's chair lay on its back, and she ran across the room and hauled him upright. Then she pulled his hood off and he blinked back at her, his face flushed with fury in the sudden light.

"Come on, let's go," Alma shouted over the screeching of metal and glass as she cut his hand restraint and pulled him to his feet. At the back of the room the door handle began to twist as someone on the far side tried to pull it open. Alma and Razer looked at each other silently, then Alma pulled Razer back towards the open window. Razer tried to speak, but before he could form a word, she had yanked him over the sill and out into the cold air.

They were in freefall for a moment, then they skidded against the cracked surface of glass and metal and began sliding downwards to the road below, spinning slowly as they went. They spilled out onto the tarmac a few seconds later, rolling across the dust and shattered glass.

In a single, fluid movement, Alma regained her feet and ran to where Reuben lay face down on the other side of the street, his head resting against the curb. It almost looked as if he was sleeping, except for the crimson streak of blood that cut across one side of the hood. Alma tore it off and turned him over. Reuben moved his head slowly towards her, his eyes streaming with terror, and tried to smile.

Around them people began to get out of their cars, blinking at the vast structure of twisted metal and glass that screeched and shuddered above them. Every few seconds it seemed to slip further into the front of the building, sending a new bank of dust and glass falling downwards, covering everything in a blanket of sparkling grey. Alma and Razer pulled Reuben across the pavement and up against the edge of the building, leaving a thick trail in the dust.

When they had reached a sheltered spot against the wall, Alma examined Reuben's bleeding ear. The lobe had torn open as he had fallen, wrapping beads of blood around the side of his head. She rolled the hood into a bundle and began dabbing the side of his face, but Reuben raised his hand to hers and touched it gently.

"Shit, I really thought...," he whispered.

"Me too," Alma said, and they held each other as more sheets of grey dust fell from the toppled building and began to pile up in great drifts across the street. Every now and then the wind would whip up eddies that skitted out beyond the next block, leaving thick grey streaks along the tarmac. The fallen building above them groaned and shuddered as its steel frame gradually folded inwards. Then there was a deafening crack as something gave way in the center of the structure, and lumps of concrete began to fall around them like giant hailstones.

"What the hell is that?" Razer said suddenly, pointing to the ground in front of them. The dust had started to shift and undulate, as if an invisible hand was stirring it against the tarmac. Razer stood and looked at the others, his face covered in white powder.

"Let's go," he seemed to say, but it was hard to hear him over the tearing noise above them. Alma pulled herself up against the wall and then helped Reuben shakily to his feet. As they stood there, Alma suddenly pointed to the ground beneath their feet. In the dust, words had begun to form.

ROYAL GRAND, ROOM 144, T

Reuben spoke first, shouting over the roaring above them. "It's Theo, I knew it." As he said the words, a sheet of concrete came crashing down in front of them.

"Come on," Razer bellowed again. They left quickly without looking back. A few blocks later they turned off the street and into the gleaming dome of a shopping mall. Half way down, Reuben suddenly stopped and turned to the others.

"Shit, that was close," he said quietly, putting his hands on either side of his head. He looked suddenly frail against the heavy gold lighting of the boutiques, and Alma touched him on the shoulder.

"Come on, we're okay now."

But Reuben held back, fear still lurking behind his eyes. "But, when we were up there, those…things said we threatened their survival." He was almost

167

whispering now, and Alma and Razor had to lean in close to hear him. "What did they mean?"

Alma frowned for a moment, staring at the floor. "Theo's code...it has opened a doorway between worlds," she said finally, pronouncing each word slowly as if thinking out loud. She looked towards the others, but it seemed as if she was gazing right through them, out to an imagined horizon. "It's as if the shared reality of the Internet, our gathered minds, have cast a shadow beyond our world, a bridge."

People had started to look at them as they stood there, covered in dust and blood.

"You of all people should see it," Alma said softly, looking across to Reuben as they started to walk again. "We live in a hyper-real world, don't we? I mean, we're connected through something that has become just as real as the physical world that surrounds us. And the financial system...well, it's another reality, one that funnels and amplifies our greed. You taught me that."

Reuben nodded as they passed out of the gold light and back onto the street.

"Shit. Of course." He stopped suddenly, holding onto the wall as the realization threw him off balance. "Every day, as we struggle to make more money, as we consume, as we try to outdo each other, all the while we project that greed and selfishness into the world we cannot see. And the shadows that live there feed off it, and it makes them stronger. And if we bring down the financial system, if we make people realize that there is more to the world than profit and loss, well then it means these shadows will just fade away. That's why they're terrified it'll end, that we'll expose this great lie that enslaves us. That's why they have crossed into our world to try to stop us." He let go of the wall and started forward again, and as he did so he began to smile.

"When the symbols of luxury lose all their meaning, when the numbers that rule us become translucent, then at last we'll be free," he declared finally as they crossed the street.

Alma buried herself into the crook of his arm while they walked through the gleaming evening, and felt a sense of peace for the first time that she could remember.

CHAPTER 28

Roxana let the cotton roll back across her skin as she slid her arms over her head and folded the pillow impatiently. She looked across the maroon and gold hotel room to where Theo sat against the skirting board, and smiled to herself as she watched him, his thick black hair clumped onion-like across the top of his head, his dark eyes flashing in the reflected light of the computer balanced on his knees. He looked up as if he sensed her watching him, and held her eyes as semi-formed thoughts passed between them across the still, warm air. At that moment, the edges of a man's voice resonated through the wall from the corridor outside, and then someone knocked impatiently against the paneled door. Roxana sat up and gathered the sheets around her in a sudden pang of apprehension.

Then Theo did something strange. Instead of opening the door, he paused, his hand against the polished handle. As Roxana watched him standing immobile on the threshold, a ghost passed fleetingly across his face. He seemed to steel himself and waited an instant for it to subside, and then dropped the latch and pulled the door free. A taller man stepped into the room and grinned through a thick beard. As the two men embraced, Roxana guessed it was Reuben.

"Fucking stupendous," the man said, pulling back. "You saved my life."

"I owed you." Theo waved the compliment away as a petite woman stepped forward and touched his elbow, her face barely visible under the hood of a tattered army coat that seemed several sizes too big. She sat down on the far side of the bed and held out a cold, pink hand from underneath the cuff.

"Hi, I'm Alma." A smile was just about visible under the frayed, green fabric as the two women shook hands. Roxana was just about to answer when she was cut short by the tinkle of glass from the other side of the room. She could just see the off-white semicircle of an untucked shirt as a third man bent forward over the minibar, rummaging impatiently among the small bottles.

"That's Razer," Alma said, flashing a knowing

smile as she shrugged off the oversize coat. "And I'm guessing you're Roxana." Then she turned to Reuben, who had pulled himself up onto a desk that ran along the end of the room. "I'm starving."

Reuben nodded. "Me too." He picked up the phone to order food.

Roxana watched Theo as they sat around and talked, surprised at how different he seemed among them. He had always been uncomfortable in groups, withdrawing to his phone, brooding alone until she rescued him with a wink. But now he seemed at ease as he talked, sitting on the end of the bed explaining how he'd seen Reuben's terror bubbling into the night, how he'd remembered the collapsed warehouse wall and had been able to push the tower block over like a giant domino.

"It just fell, it wasn't even difficult," he was saying as he caught Roxana's eye and smiled.

"Man, no one can touch us now," Reuben shouted, but Razor cut him short.

"Don't be so sure, mate," he said from the armchair on the other side of the room, over-emphasizing the words as he placed an empty glass down on the fabric. "I mean, who knows what they can do?"

Theo glanced up at Roxana quickly; she looked startled.

"Who? Who does he mean?" she said quickly, but at that moment steaming boxes of pizza arrived, and there was silence in the room as Reuben paid and they all began to eat. It wasn't until they had almost finished that Reuben turned to answer her, choosing his words carefully.

"Look, we're close, we're really close to shutting down the financial system and putting an end to the lies that society feeds us every day." Roxana nodded and smiled. "But...." He lowered his voice as if he feared being overheard. "But, there are people, things, trying to stop us. It's like by using the Internet they've found a way to cross from the shadow world that surrounds us into the real, physical world." He tapped the top of the dresser as he spoke.

"I've seen them," Theo said suddenly. "I mean, really seen them. When I went back there, when Reuben was falling. They ran from me." He leaned forward. "They were terrified of me there."

"But not here." Reuben gestured around the room, and they all fell silent for a while, lost in thought, until Alma spoke again.

"Shit, we need to act. I mean, we can't wait for them to come here." Roxana shuddered as she spoke.

Reuben walked over to the window and pulled back the thick curtain to look down into the street. "We can wait for them over there. We've still got the

code that Razer left hidden for us inside the system."
He nodded at Razer, who didn't seem to hear and
was staring intently into the bottom of the empty
glass. "We just need to activate it, but to do it one
of us needs to stay here." Reuben looked up at the
others and Alma met his gaze, her eyes soft in the
low light.

"Man, I'll do it," she said slowly.

"We'll be able to see where you are. We'll be
right there…they won't be able to touch you."

He stepped back into the center of the room. As
he did so, the glass Razer had been holding rolled
off the arm of the chair and onto the floor. Reuben
looked up and realized he had fallen asleep, his head
lolling over the side of the chair.

"Good idea," he said, and Alma nodded. The
adrenalin that had fueled them over the past few days
had begun to subside with the weight of the food and
the still warmth of the hotel room. "We'll do it in the
morning," Reuben muttered as he lay down on the
floor next to the bed and pulled his black coat over
him, his boots sticking out of the end awkwardly.

CHAPTER 29

She watched the battle between light and dark as it waged back and forth across the rippled surface, dark holding sway only for a moment until a wave of yellow light came crashing in with the hiss of the next passing car. Alma paused, suspended on the threshold between sleep and wakefulness, as her thoughts coalesced gradually in the dim light. She became aware of the weight of the bed covers across her body, and the pressure of an elbow embedded into her back. She twisted her head carefully towards the stack of yellow curls that fell across the pillow, and tried to push Roxana's arm back. But the edge of the bed was too close and she couldn't get the purchase, so she rotated the other way and looked out to where the darkness pooled onto the floor like

175

water.

Alma could just make out Reuben as he lay under his greatcoat, breathing hard into a pillow he had folded under his head. She eased along the edge of the mattress and lowered herself carefully off the end of the bed and onto the floor. It was cold now, and she pulled on her coat and stood for a moment in the darkness, listening to the others as they slept. Then she stepped across to the narrow desk at the end of the room, scooped the heavy plastic fob of the hotel key into her pocket, and stepped out into the hallway.

The electric lights hummed urgently as she made her way past the anonymous doors, each one set slightly back from the corridor. She had half hoped that there would be a food machine next to the grey metal panels of the lift doors, but it wasn't that kind of hotel. Alma sank her finger into the gilded button on the wall and let it rest there for a moment, the noise of the electric lights leaching into her mind like an unwelcome thought as she waited. The muted ping that marked the arrival of the car came almost too fast, as if it had been pre-warned. As she descended, Alma watched herself in the mirror, her face looking back suspiciously from under the heavy green hood. By the time she reached the darkened lobby, her sense of unease had become shrill.

She made her way quickly across the floor to the main desk and stood there stupidly. Something was wrong. Alma craned over the glossy wood in case the night clerk was busy there in the shadows, but the unnatural darkness seemed to absorb her thoughts for a moment, and then Alma realized that the sound of traffic outside had ceased.

She passed through the overlapping shadows to the front door and looked out onto the empty street, where thick droplets of rain had started to fall. The darkness along the edge of the building seemed to shift and move as she watched, and then it formed into rows of black helmets crouching there. Alma recoiled, her heart lurching inside her ribcage as she staggered backwards through the mottled light. When she reached the far wall she saw the hotel door swing silently open. The counter blocked her view, but she could imagine the men crouching as they poured into the lobby.

She tried not to breathe as she moved sideways into the stairwell, and then she ran up the dark wooden staircase, almost blind with panic. When she reached her floor she paused, listening for a moment before stepping out onto the landing. She had only made it a few paces when the treacherous noise of the lift car rang out behind her, and she slipped sideways into one of the narrow alcoves and breathed in hard.

Alma could hear lowered voices now as the men spoke urgently, and then the sound of boots. She held her breath, fear clearing the thoughts from her mind like a cold wind. Then a man was standing in front of her, the light playing across the ridges of his sheer black clothing, his face grim under the rough cloth. The head turned slowly, and for an instant he and Alma looked at each other silently.

"Here," he shouted finally, his voice uncertain. Alma sensed that he was scared too as he reached out to grab her arm, and she pushed the black glove aside gently and ran. Behind her, she could hear the deadly grating of metal against metal as weapons were readied. She closed her eyes, bracing herself.

Then there was a crack and she stumbled, waiting for an explosion of pain. But none came, and she regained her balance clumsily and looked back. The carpet hung behind her in torn strips over a concrete shard that pushed out of the floor like a broken bone. A fine dust was falling, covering the men in white as they stood against the wall, looking around in disarray. The paintings that hung along the corridor wall began to sway violently. Then the whole corridor shuddered, and lumps of plaster began to fall from the ceiling. The men fell onto each other as the walls on either side of them buckled inwards, sending the pictures crashing to the floor.

In the din Alma fumbled with the lock, her hands shaking, and then stepped into the room and let the door swing shut behind her.

It looked empty, the bed covers thrown back, Razor's chair on its side. Alma took several paces forward before she noticed the top of Reuben's head against the far side of the mattress. She rounded the bed quickly, and saw the four of them sitting along the edge. But they did not acknowledge her, and Alma bent down in the gloom to examine Reuben. His face was vacant, his eyes half closed, the eyeballs rolled upwards as he looked at an unseen landscape, his pale skin flickering in the weak light of a laptop that was open on the floor in front of them.

She stepped back, and then she noticed another computer that stood waiting on the desk at the far end, a cursor flashing patiently. She understood immediately, and prepared to activate the code that lay waiting for her in the heart of the system.

CHAPTER 30

Reuben had heard them first as he lay on the floor half dreaming, and had woken in a panic and gathered the others, drowsy and confused, around the computer. It was Reuben who had let the code take them stumbling into time's antechamber, and out into the ruined building to break down the walls that supported the ancient corridor where Alma stood cornered.

But it was Razer who had come breathless, his face shimmering in the thick air as they waited in the hotel room for Alma to inch forwards through time. "There's something you need to see." His eyes had burned with fury as he spoke. "I've found a way to end all of this." The final syllable elongated and merged with the sound of a storm that had picked up outside. But Roxana held back, her face folded in worry.

"Aren't we supposed to be here, for her?" She'd waved her arm towards the hotel room, which was empty now except a broken chair, leaning strutless on one side against the peeling wall where the half-formed phrases of Alma's thoughts echoed. "Me and Theo could stay, just in case," Roxana had said, but Razer cut her short.

"No." The force of the word surprised the others. "None of this matters anymore, but we need to hurry." He'd moved backwards into the corridor, the light from his body scattering the shadows that lingered there. Reuben, Theo, and Roxana looked at each other for a moment, unsure. Then Reuben had stepped after him into the geometric shafts of light that danced along the peeling walls, and the others had followed uncertainly.

Razer led them back along the corridor, over the strips of fallen plaster and broken picture frames, and into the stairwell. They wound upwards into the shell of the derelict building as it shook and shivered with the violence of the storm outside. As they advanced, flashes of electric blue lightning caught their faces momentarily, their expressions dark with apprehension. Every now and then they passed a glassless window, and through the broken frames they caught glimpses of the black sky seething and boiling overhead.

But nothing could have prepared them for what was to come as they stepped through the final door that led to the upper floor, the towering blackness they could see through the gaps where the walls and ceiling had started to collapse. As they stood in the center of the room like miniature figurines, an immense vortex coiled around them, its sheer walls bubbling, black with dark souls that had converged around the derelict hotel. They stood huddled in the broken canopy of the upper floor, speechless before the vast tornado.

Suddenly Razer began to walk backwards away from the center of the room. When he reached the doorway he paused, his hair suspended around his head in the circling wind, his contorted face flashing blue from the lightning that forked along the walls of the vortex.

"I'm sorry," he shouted, his voice distorted in the damp, heavy air. "But they promised me that I'll be powerful again." Then he stepped back and closed the door on them as thunder rippled through the heavy air.

Reuben ran across the room and threw his shoulder into the crumbling wood, propelling his bodyweight forward. But as he did so, the black wall of the vortex closed in, the howling wind pinning the door closed. He looked backwards at the others desperately, and then he pushed his shoulder into the wall next to him, expecting to roll forward into the empty space beyond the edge of the building. But the black wall of the vortex folded in again and held the crumbling brickwork fast. Theo joined him and together they pushed against the ancient masonry, but it did not move. The vortex had tightened around the frame of the building now, and Reuben turned his head upward, his face flashing as lightning streaked overhead, and howled into the black cone of the sky.

CHAPTER 31

There they stood, frozen in time as the darkness pressed in around them, the sheer walls swirling around the edges of the derelict hotel, the small disk of sky narrowing overhead. The outlines of Roxana's face seemed artificial in the flickering light, like a paper cut-out, her eyes wide and black as she looked at the other two across the empty room and screamed. Theo held her as small flakes began to tear from the walls and strafe against their faces.

"There's no hope for us now," Theo shouted over the wind. He seemed to have grown taller as he spoke, his voice deepening. He gestured to the hordes of black souls that shrieked and swirled in the darkness outside. As the seething walls of the vortex finally closed in overhead, blocking out the sky completely, he looked down at them and shouted into the gloom, "We could have destroyed them, but now we are lost."

"No." Reuben was standing directly underneath a hole in the center of the roof, his hair coiling around his head, serpentine in the swirling air, his face flickering blue prophetically as lighting crackled overhead. "Our love will save us, it's the only thing we have now."

Roxana suddenly pulled Theo against her, their lips pressed together as flashes of amber began to stream up into the blackness. A second later, a ray of light cut through the shadows. Behind them the door tore away from the wall and spiraled into the storm. A glowing figure stood in the empty frame, throwing gold light out across the broken floor. Reuben rushed forward for the opening, and then faltered, momentarily lost as he stood there looking into a familiar face framed in dreadlocks.

"Zed, what the fuck?"

The face in the doorway cracked into a wide smile. "I knew you would come," Zed said as he stepped into the room. "But I've been waiting so long."

"But...." Theo faltered, confused. "I mean, where the hell did you go?"

Zed's smile faded and his eyed darkened as

the wind howled against the open doorway. "They killed me man," Zed said, his voice distorting as he bellowed over the storm, unable to look up and meet their eyes. "I didn't see anything, all I know is this." He pointed at the side of his neck, where a thick black line passed just under his Adam's apple and then curved horrifically upwards to his ear on the other side. "Since I died I've been here in this shadow world, waiting for you." As he spoke, the storm tore a piece of wood from the roof and sent it clattering against the wall behind them, and Roxana grabbed Theo's sleeve.

"We need to go," she shouted, pulling him backwards towards the door as the wind howled around them.

"Wait." Theo resisted, holding her back as another section of the ceiling crashed to the floor next to them. "How did you find us?" He looked back at Zed, who was gazing mesmerized through the broken ceiling at the tunnel of darkness that gyrated far above them. "Zed." Theo pulled on Zed's hooded top, the same one he had been wearing in the squat all those weeks ago, and Zed looked down at him, a strange expression flashing across his face. "How did you find us? I mean, how did you know we were here?"

Zed smiled, and as he did so the light emanating

from him intensified, and for a moment they could see that the ancient walls of the room had started to crack under the pressure of the storm overhead.

"But it was your kiss," Zed bellowed, looking up at Roxana, who stood in the doorway. "I saw it from across the city." He gestured over the wall. "And I knew it was you."

"For God's sake, Alma needs us. Let's go," Roxana shouted again. By now the wind was so strong that she struggled to stand, and she held onto the lintel with both hands. Theo stepped towards her, and then looked back into the room.

"Reuben, where the hell is Reuben?"

"Don't worry," Zed's shouted back, his face turned upwards again towards the vortex. "He's already gone."

CHAPTER 32

Reuben had left as soon as the door opened, spiraling downwards into the dark, vibrating building to where Alma had been poised to destroy the system. When he got there the corridor was black with shadows, its walls glistening and dank. With silent fury he plunged towards the open doorway, the darkness parting ahead of him. Black figures crowded around Alma, projecting dark-faced attackers into the hotel room. Reuben could hear her screaming now, and he shook with fury as he pushed in amongst them, tearing them back. Then he stood over the place where she lay and threw his arms open, roaring into the whistling air as light from his body filled the room. The shadows around him hissed and chattered in the sudden brightness and fled, pouring through the doorway behind him like drain water. In the calm that followed, he could hear Alma calling his name across the void, and for a moment their thoughts overlapped and tangled as he waited for her to push her hand forward through time and release the code.

She must have still been holding the computer, because it didn't take long. There was a small spark in the air underneath Reuben as she pressed the button, and then a shockwave rolled up through the building to the roof.

***

The shockwave passed along Theo's body as he stood in the eye of the storm, and out into the thick air. It tore a ring through the bottom of the vortex, leaving filaments floating like pieces of fabric. For a moment there was calm, in the same way that a tidal wave first pulls back the sea to reveal the silent, glistening sands. And then it came, crashing back over them, a pulse that parted the sky and peeled back the towering black walls into thick ribbons that coiled away and dissolved into the light that had broken through. The building was shaking violently, and behind Theo and Roxana, a long panel of roof collapsed, pulling the frail walls of the atrium inwards.

"You need to go." Zed's face had swelled, and

189

now he hung above them in the air. Theo glanced back into the cavern of the stairwell as the roof on top of it cracked and bricks began to clatter down the steps. "He'll be okay, you must go now." Theo looked into Zed's black eyes as plaster crashed around them. "See you again, my friend." Zed held out his hand and Theo reached across to touch it. Their palms overlapped, occupying for a moment the same location in space, then the floor underneath Theo shuddered violently and he ran over to the edge of the building. For an instant Theo and Roxana stood on the cornice as small dark threads streamed past, caught in the updraft. He held her to him and kissed her as they closed their eyes and stepped out into the torrent. Theo's black coat wrapped itself around them as they floated slowly downwards.

Then as they touched the ground, everything suddenly fell quiet, and Theo could feel a cool breeze against his skin. He opened his eyes and blinked, golden daylight blinding him for an instant. He could hear the murmur of passing traffic, and overhead the gentle rustle of swaying trees. Commuters streamed around them as they held each other without speaking in the oblivious, still morning. Theo turned back towards the hotel entrance just as Reuben and Alma walked through the heavy wooden doorway and out into the street. Reuben looked up and held

Theo's gaze for a moment in the sudden calm, and then they stepped out into the anonymous flow of people and disappeared from sight.

Behind them Theo could see a row of ATMs flickering unnaturally as the geometric patterns on the screens distorted and then faded into black, and he smiled to himself as he took Roxana by the hand and turned away into the welcoming light of the early morning sun.

I had my first computer when I was 18. The one after that was connected to the internet, although I was the only one of my friends with a dial-up connection for at least a year. I remember my first multimedia PC, my first polyphonic ring tone, and wondering why anyone would want a camera on a telephone.

I've always been fascinated by technology and the impact it is having on our lives. It's why I have worked as a technology journalist for the past 15 years, and it's why I chose computer hacking as the subject of my first novel, Translucence. I am currently working on a follow-up.